Special thanks to my dear friends ~~Carol Stanley and Molly Burke!~~

"George Arau has written a beautiful tribute to his brother. When he came to me to edit his book it was obvious from the very beginning that this was deeply personal work inspired by love. He worked with such dedication and passion to create a story that would honor the memory of his brother. It is such a moving, wonderful work and George toiled tirelessly to perfect it. My wish for him is that now that he has given the book to the world his heart will truly mend. It is a generous book that tells us all that in giving to others we can heal ourselves. I was honored to work with George and I hope he will always be my friend."

Carol Stanley

"Something about George's vision for the work, and his passion to help others was very moving to me as we began to work on the project, and I decided to give the novel some of my time. Once I began, I couldn't put the novel down. I fell in love with the book to this day I can't drive down Van Nuys Boulevard without thinking about all the characters in LOST PIGEONS. They have become like family to me, and I treasure having gotten to know and care about them all."

Molly Berke

LOST PIGEONS

A Novel

George Arau

*One man's guilt puts him
on a quest to save a homeless man's life
after he fails to save his own brother.*

Library of Congress Cataloging-in-Publication Data
LOST PIGEONS by George Arau

1. George Arau. 2. Lost Pigeons. 3. Van Nuys. 4. PTSD.
5. Suicide. 6. Homelessness.

ISBN-13: 978-1-0957-1622-9

Printed in the USA.

For more information about bulk sales or promotional pricing,
please contact us!
Contact: George Arau, E-mail: georgedinla@yahoo.com.

This book may be purchased from the author. Please inquire as to costs for shipping.

Table of Contents

Prologue   7

Chapter 1: The Life of Boys   11

Chapter 2: Curfews and Adolescence   24

Chapter 3: Malibu   58

Chapter 4: Michael   74

Chapter 5: Ricky's World   85

Chapter 6: Aftermath   109

Chapter 7: Searching   124

Chapter 8: Sales Meeting   129

Chapter 9: Merry Christmas   134

Chapter 10: The Lady in White   145

Chapter 11: The Only Way Out is Through   160

Chapter 12: Redemption   175

Prologue

HIS HANDS RUBBED the well-worn leather binding of the photo album. He took another sip of Johnnie Walker whiskey and flipped through the pages until he came to the photo of a handsome young man dressed in all the trappings of war. He put his hands over his brother's image, as if to somehow will his brother's energy to come through the stillness of the page into his own body. He shook his head. Why? Why? A tear fell on his brother's picture. He wiped it away quickly with his shirtsleeve, afraid the teardrop would somehow wash away his brother's face. His wife was in their bed when she heard it.

"Damn it! Why? Why? Why did you have to do this? Why?" he yelled as he stomped around the kitchen. He was in that state of inebriation in which things are repeated over and over and over again.

"Michael?" she quietly called out to her husband. She came down the stairs, stepping softly. "Don't wake up the girls," she said in hushed tones. "C'mon, honey. It's 2 A.M. and you've been down here for hours. Come to bed."

"Leave me alone," he said, knocking back his drink.

"But honey, you have to get some rest. You've got work in the morning."

"Just leave me alone. You will never understand!" he answered.

"I do understand how deeply this pain has wounded you. I'd have to be blind not to see what this has done to you. And I'm worried about you. It's about your drinking. I wish… I wish you'd stop." It was only a breath, not said as an accusation, but an expression of love and concern.

Now with watery eyes, he took out a matchbook from his front shirt pocket and gently stroked the well-worn cover. "Remember this?" he said, holding the matchbook with his thumb and forefinger so that his wife could see.

"Let me see," said his wife. "Ah. A matchbook."

"Much more than that," he said, opening the matchbook for her to see. Inside was a picture of his brother, young and smiling.

"Remember this?" he asked again.

"Um. I don't know," she confessed.

"You don't remember when Stephanie… I just can't believe this. This… this is from our daughter. Our daughter… in second grade. Don't you remember? Surely you remember." He was slurring now. "You see, something of value had to be brought to school, something very precious to each child so they could create something of it, a real treasure to bring home. And our Stephanie, our beautiful, beautiful Stephanie, you remember what she did? Instead of money, gold or jewelry, she made this, something she made with her own hands. She made a little treasure box and she… put his picture in it, to never forget him. She really loved him, you know. We all loved him! I don't understand why he had to go like that. He left us!"

There was a long pause between them. Then his wife very gently put her hand on his cheek and looked up at him, speaking softly. "I understand what you're going through, I really do. I wish I could change it for you. I wish I could take away all the pain, but I can't. Only time can do that, darling… only time. I thought the worst of it might be gone by now, but I see the wound needs more time to heal. Put down the drink, darling. Alcohol can't take your grief away. But it can take away everything we have here. We have a life here… now. We have built something together. We have two beautiful girls to raise, and I promise you that he will never be forgotten. Just put down the drink and come with me. This isn't you, Michael." She embraced him tenderly.

Michael, with tears in his eyes, said again, "Why? Why did he have to go like that? There is no God! And if there is one, I hate him!"

"You can tell God how much you hate him in the morning. I love you; let me help you get upstairs in bed."

Upstairs, one of the girls began to cry. "Mommy!"

"I'm coming," she said.

"Did I wake her up?" Michael said, whispering and crying at the same time.

"No, she probably had a nightmare. Just come with me," she said, taking his hand and leading him toward the stairs.

"I'm sorry, my love," he said, now in the remorseful phase of intoxication. "Forgive me, and thank you for putting up with me. I'm such a..."

"Hush, darling," she breathed, leading him toward their bedroom. "I love you."

Chapter 1

The Life of Boys

S OME OF MY memories, I see as if I am looking through
fog or gauze. They morph and change and have soft edg-
es that bleed into the dark corners of my mind. Others are
so clear, it's as though they were shot in HD. I play them
over and over, running them over obsessively as though if I
run them often enough, I might catch something that would
change the outcome. What I remember very clearly is that my
brother Chris always had my back.

I remember an autumn that came to Sherman Oaks not
with the flutter of an occasional leaf, but with an intense, blaz-
ing heat, the highest on record in three years, a hundred de-

grees and not a breeze anywhere in the San Fernando Valley. Fire weather. It made you tense, on edge and unsettled. You could smell the heat and see it rising in waves off the pavement that made the air ripple and blur. There was drought, and many a lawn had since given up the ghost. The only hope for some shade was at the park. We just had to practice football despite my mother's admonitions about heatstroke and instructions to keep applying sunblock and drink Gatorade.

We were kids. We were young. We were playful and maybe ridiculous and without a care, as is appropriate for young boys. You grow up fast enough; and adulthood, with its heavy mantle of responsibility and reality, swallows you whole, like critical ground failure. We all live on a fault, betting against all odds that we won't be one of the victims when the inevitable Big One finally hits in whatever form.

Bobby was the jester in our group. He tried out all his dumbest jokes on us, as in, "Satan called. He wants his weather back! He wants his weather back. Get it? Weather!" And he'd roll on the ground, laughing at his own joke. Why I remember that after all these years, I don't know. I asked him if, because he was such a jerk with his truly bad jokes, he had the heatstroke my mother had warned us about.

"Definitely," Chris said. "Bobby, you're on the bench." Chris was the quarterback and captain. He was always the leader.

"But there is no bench. There's only grass."

"Your ass is grass, then."

"Aw, man!" Bobby kicked the dirt, but he sat down in the grass on the sidelines.

Despite the punishing heat, we were determined to practice. We faced each other in formation, two on two, with determination. When I think back on it now, the grimness makes me smile. We were all practically blinded by the sweat dripping from our foreheads into our eyes, but we didn't care.

"HUT!" I looked behind me. Chris was there, solid as the Rock of Gibraltar.

"HUT!" A fly buzzed around Chris's golden-tinged eyelashes, but he would not be distracted. One of the heavier guys, Bruce, kneeling opposite him, shifted his position and growled at my brother. But Chris didn't care. He was faster. He just flashed his white teeth at Bruce.

"So?" he said, spat into the grass, and crouched deeper, ready for the ball.

"HIKE!" I snapped. Chris, with what he called his "Amazing Hands of Wonder," caught the ball in a flash, and tucked the little pigskin under his arm like a baby. Like lightning, he slipped through the linebackers opposite him like he was coated head-to-toe with Parkay margarine.

I stood up to see if he made it through the offensive line, and Bruce flattened me.

One minute, I was standing; and the next, I woke up to Chris shaking me, repeating over and over,

"Mikey! Mikey! You all right?"

Bruce was standing at my feet, nursing a shiner, sniffling that he didn't mean to do it.

Chris, with a look that could freeze fire, told him,

"You ever so much as touch a hair on Mikey's head again, I'll blacken both eyes so you have a matched pair, you brainless blob of fat!" He was shorter than Bruce, but what he lacked in stature, he made up for in sheer gutsiness.

Bruce taunted him, "Yeah, why don't you take care of your little sister, then, Chrissy-wissy?"

"Chrissy-wissy?" Chris drew back his fist to hit him, but when he slugged at Bruce, he missed. Chris scratched his head and laughed. Who knew? Bruce runs pretty fast… for a fat guy.

We both watched Bruce fade into the distance. Then I laughed, and we decided it would be in our best interest not to let my mother know I'd been knocked cold.

A couple of years later, we were still trick-or-treating, even though we were probably too old. But we hung onto it just for the fun, definitely for the candy, and maybe to hold on just a little longer to our fast-fleeting childhood.

I remember the sound of my brother's voice saying "Trick or Treat!" It sounded strange to me because he had this squeaky, new baritone. We cleaned up that year, and met our friends to count our spoils and compare and trade. Tim definitely had the biggest surprise. He held up a bottle of Mogen David 20/20, a fortified wine way too strong for the likes of us who had never even tasted alcohol. It was also called Mad Dog, and it lived up to its name. Tim told us crazy old Mr. Chandler had given it to him. Thinking back on it, it was a truly crazy thing Chandler had done, giving alcohol to a kid. My father, had he known, would have been irate.

We'd pitched a six-man tent in our backyard that year; and with our friends, we planned on scaring the hell out of one another with ghost stories. The moon was full, but clouds drifted over it so the darkness was thick and ominous all around us. Or at least, we thought it was and made it so because we wanted it to be.

My mother and father neither hovered over us nor neglected us. They intuitively found just the right balance, and always made our friends feel welcome. That Halloween night, my mother, Mimi, brought out blankets and comforters for our friends; and made us all burgers and a special burrito for Tim, accommodating him because he was a vegetarian. I was too young to appreciate the ease and good cheer with which she did this. We had the unfettered, free life of boys whose parents loved them and let them run just wild enough. I guess in some ways, it was idyllic, but of course you only know those things later when you'd like to recapture the feeling and it's gone forever.

I didn't realize at the time, along with many other things, that my mother was really quite lovely with her shoulder-length curly brown hair, her fair skin and oval face. She was tall and slender, kind and thoughtful, and a damn good cook. She and my father made one another happy, which I think was why we had a happy home that was full of life and friends and backyard barbecues. We felt contented and safe. That was until the testosterone kicked in and we became restless as though we had an itch to scratch that we couldn't quite reach, Chris first then me a couple of years later. It was only later that I understood that both my mother and father had given us both a really wonderful childhood.

But I guess we didn't hold onto it long enough because after everyone had eaten, we'd crowded around the television to watch *The Great Pumpkin*.

Then we really got down to business.

We sat in a circle in the tent. Tim yelled,

"Treats!"

I, being the youngest there and perhaps a bit more innocent than the others, thought he meant "let's break out all the candy". But he meant something else entirely. He held up the bottle.

Chris, who was always the leader, said he knew just how were going to do this. We'd go around the circle, each telling part of a ghost story. After each turn, we'd take a swig of the Mad Dog.

I wasn't sure, but I followed my brother's lead. He had never given me any reason to mistrust him. In fact, I'd always looked up to him, even though I would never have told him so.

In our day to day, we miss so many cues. We often miss those things that would give us insight into the true nature of a situation or someone we love. But that night, I perceived a kind of wildness in my brother I had failed to recognize before, though at that age I could not put it into words. It was but a momentary glimpse of a certain recklessness that I would look back on years later with clarity I would have preferred never to have had.

Tim loved the idea, and yelled that we'd all be mad dogs! Since it was his bottle, he went first, starting with a story about a boy named Michael who was lost in the woods, alone at night. Tim probably knew this would make me the most scared.

Then Bobby started.

"He was alone and defenseless. He could hear something creeping toward him. He could hear it breathing, but he couldn't see it. Whatever the thing was, it wasn't something from this world. He could feel it near him." Then he took a drink.

The others took their turns, and I guess we all really wanted to be scared. And with the added Mad Dog magic, it wasn't hard to imagine that every sound was something ominous. Everyone was full of alcohol-fueled bravado and unease at the same time. But no one was more uneasy than me.

Chris went last. With the flashlight held under his face, he looked distorted and frightening. I could feel this invisible thing touching the back of my neck. He suddenly touched the back of my neck, and I think I might have screamed. Then he took a swig from the bottle, then a second one. "I'm a mad dog, a mad, mad, mad, dog!" he said, and he hopped up and did a crazy, mad-dog dance, then he threw back his head and howled.

I could feel the invisible thing all around me; it was all over me. It made my skin crawl. We heard a twig snap behind him, and a horrible laugh and something with a voice that sounded like wind and old dry leaves said, "You'll never leave this forest alive." When I looked back, I couldn't see anything. It was pitch-black.

Then I heard something real coming from outside the tent. I was petrified when the others heard it, too. I would have been far less terror-stricken had it been only my imagination. It was a long, mournful, slow howl.

Then came another, and another. Then... Silence. All of us held our breath, waiting for another sound. The deep silence was more frightening than the howling. We were all hyper-alert, waiting, just waiting.

Chris told me to zip up the tent, but I couldn't move. He got up and secured it. Then he picked up his aluminum baseball bat and swung it over his head; and always the leader, he told the others that he "had this."

We were young and free, and the alcohol made us a little wild, and we did the things kids do. With alcohol for fortitude, Chris decided that it was time to leave the tent and have some serious fun. We were going to TP the school. And armed with a dozen rolls, what a job we did. The school looked as if it had been attacked by a giant carton of Charmin. When the debauchery was over with, we all stood back to admire the handiwork.

That was when Sally Bond, the most popular girl in eighth grade, walked up to us with her super-popular friends. I guess it was the first time I registered that my brother was seriously interested in girls. He was swaying a little because he'd had so much to drink, but he was coherent.

Sally asked about what happened. Chris, with a lot of charm for a kid, told her he had "nooooooooooo" idea. None. We'd just arrived. Sally was a pretty redhead and Chris was definitely flirting, and he didn't care if we all saw it. He knew no one would make fun of him. No one ever made fun of my brother. But Sally looked at him and looked at the school, and you could tell she knew we were responsible for the public art we'd made of the school. We were caught in the act, and fell all over one another as we beat a hasty retreat.

We did the crazy things boys sometimes do in the course of growing up, but we'd never really been in trouble. So my parents were surprised to be summoned to school.

Principal Jacob was not amused. He sat and looked at me and Chris over the top of his horn-rimmed glasses, his salt-and-pepper crew cut shiny like the bristles of a porcupine. He was a tough but fair man who didn't take any malarkey off of anyone.

I remember my mother uncrossed her legs, and primly sat straight up, not looking at us. She was so mortified. My father, dressed in his best suit, would not sit down. He couldn't stop clearing his throat, or shifting from one foot to the other. He had hold of the back of Chris's chair, and was squeezing it for all it was worth.

After what seemed an eternity, the Principal spoke.

"I just don't know what has gotten into you boys. I have never had you in my office, either one of you! What made you take part in this vandalism? I know there were others. Who were they?"

We were both silent and did not look up at him. He shook his head, looking over the paperwork that sat in the school's permanent records on top of his desk. He held up a picture. "This, is this funny?"

I answered, "No, sir," but Chris was silent. I knew he had a colossal hangover and could barely stand the sound of a feather on glass, much less an interrogation by the principal with our parents present.

The principal "let us off easy." We had detention until the end of the year, lunch duty until the end of the summer, and of course my father grounded us "for the foreseeable future." I suppose it was what would now be called a "teachable moment."

But time passed; and despite our constant rounds of chores and detention after what became known as the Mogen David incident, we had a good autumn, or what passed for autumn in Southern California. We had the lives of boys who came from a loving home. The holidays came. My mother prepared an enormous traditional Thanksgiving feast, with turkey and dressing and apple pie for dessert. She made the best apple pie anywhere, ever.

I remember the day Chris showed me how to shave. "See, you have to go smoothly around the edge of the face, like so," said Chris, "or you'll cut your nose off." He flicked the double-bladed razor in the sink, and it flashed in the bathroom light like a thunderbolt. He unloaded a pile of shaving cream into the cold tap water. I was in awe as Chris held his mouth in just the right position and shaved a swath of white lather from cheekbone to chin.

"Wow," I said. "But aren't you afraid you'll cut yourself?"

"No, don't be a dummy," said Chris. "Besides, dad taught me."

I was playing with the old-fashioned shaving brush and cup dad had given Chris when he turned 18. It was a family tradition. Chris finished shaving and looked me in the eye. "This double-bladed razor gives the cleanest shave. See?" And Chris wiped the excess shaving cream off the finished side of his face. "Smooth as a baby's bottom!" He grinned, faking a bad British accent, and gesturing for me to stroke his cheek.

I reached up and gave my brother a smack on the cheek instead. Chris was stunned for a minute.

"Oh, you are a brave, brave man now, aren't ya?" Chris said.

I just stood there stuttering for a moment, shocked at myself for how stupidly, stupidly brave I had just been.

"This is the part where you would want to run." said Chris.

I said, "I'm-a-I'm-a..."

Chris counted down, "3-2-1..."

I turned tail and ran. Chris turned in hot pursuit behind me. As we thundered down the hallway, with him quickly catching up with me, mamma called out from the kitchen,

"Boys! Boys! You know what dad says about running in the house! Come get washed up for supper!"

We were in the backyard by the time she finished her sentence. We were on the ground, wrestling. But I heard her say "Oh, I tell you. Those boys will be the death of me, I swear." It's something we often gave her cause to say.

Mimi, our mother, often thought that perhaps time went faster the older you got. To her, it seemed she just blinked, and we went from junior high to high school. And now, with another blink, one of us would leave the nest soon.

Christmases and birthdays flew by. We put on weight, got taller, and bloomed into young men right before her eyes, faster than you could say "Jack in the Beanstalk". That's what she said. The tiny babies turned into beanstalks before her eyes. It wasn't fair to a mother, the stealing of time, the stealing of the precious cuddles in infancy to the "don't touch me" of young adulthood, to what would soon be an empty house. Well, except for Bill, our dad. "Good old Bill," she would sigh as she washed the dishes.

Our lives returned to normal, to the ordinary rhythms of school and homework and sports. Growing up, we bantered and tried to one-up one another; and sometimes, we fought as siblings do. When my mother admonished us, we stopped for a moment or two, then started up again. And when she gave us motherly advice – use sunblock, wear a hat, put on a jacket, etc., we would roll our eyes or signal with secret hand gestures about how funny we thought it was. It was a stable home with warmth, affection and laughter.

My father could put his foot down simply by saying our names in a certain tone: "Michael!" or "Chris!", or sometimes "You two!" That would stop our dubious behavior, be it teasing, roughhousing, or arguing with our mother. I'm not sure what would have happened if we had persisted in whatever behavior he was curtailing. He had presence and an air of authority, but he never abused it as he was at heart a kind and decent man who loved us. We were in a sense unremarkable, in the way that Tolstoy said all happy families are alike.

My brother was always the star athlete. He was the quarterback of our high school football team. Everyone knew him. You would have thought life would open up to him and embrace him as he went forward.

My parents gave us both great affection. We tolerated our mother's frequent hugs because we loved her, but only for a fleeting moment. And now one of us was getting ready to graduate. We laughed when she gave us her theories on time. We were young, and we had all the time in the world.

Chapter 2

Curfews and Adolescence

A T OUR SCHOOL, the junior and senior proms were held together. I might have been only a sophomore, but Chris set me up with a girl in the junior class who, according to him, thought I was cute and agreed to go with me. My mother and father questioned my going along as I was two years younger. But Chris, who was driving his ultra-cool convertible that he'd saved up for through a little lawn-maintenance business we'd put up together, promised he would look after me.

My father looked as though he thought this claim was flimsy at best.

"I was young once, you know. I remember what it's like," he said. But he gave his permission.

And so the night arrived. I was nervous and checked myself in the mirror a hundred times. It had never been this important to me in the past, but prom night magnified hundredfold the self-consciousness that is part of the adolescence package, which made my brother laugh. He seemed totally self-assured. He was graced with the looks of the lead singers and movie stars whose pictures hung on the walls of teenage girls. He had grown into his looks and seemed to possess a confidence I lacked.

When we took the beautiful orchid corsages we had bought for our dates, my mother became misty-eyed and sentimental.

"Beautiful. Just beautiful," she said, hugged us both as if there was no tomorrow, and told us how much she loved us, something neither of us ever doubted for a single moment. My father said the corsages were beautiful, too; but he had other things on his mind – laying down the rules. He lowered his voice, which is what he always did when he talked to us about something he deemed serious; and the rules for the night, he deemed very serious. Treat the girls with respect; honor the curfew set by their family; don't have them home a minute later; and absolutely no drinking, and in particular, no drinking and driving. He looked straight at Chris and was silent until my brother nodded that he understood.

There was yet another round of hugs and kisses from my mother as she dried her tears on a dishtowel. Then we were off in my brother's car, with Chris bellowing a wild war hoop while cranking the radio to maximum volume and peeling out of our driveway, sending pebbles flying with a screeching of tires that I am sure caused my father to feel that he had not laid down the rules forcefully enough.

My self-consciousness had followed me into the car and sat close beside me, leaving little room for anything else. The date Chris had arranged for me was from the popular crowd I always thought was out of my league. It occurred to me that maybe Charlotte, my date, was just doing my brother a favor and really had no interest in me. But there was little time to gnaw on this troubling thought as the girls lived almost within walking distance, and it seemed we were there as soon as we left our driveway. I sat in my seat and made no move to get out of the car.

My brother asked what was wrong with me, and I pointed out to him that these girls were really popular. He looked at me for a moment and asked,

"What do you think we are?"

I hesitated, he called me a dork, and I punched him in his arm, things that brothers do.

"C'mon, you're gonna have a great time, a real adventure. Now get outta the freaking car... now." We pulled up to Charlotte's house. "Ready?"

"Ready as I'll ever be," I said, clearing my throat. The damned tie was choking me. Chris got out of the car and straightened his suit. He pushed open the gate. I was still checking out my reflection in the car window.

"You coming?" he asked.

"Uh, yeah," I answered. I pushed my way past the front gate, snagging my shoulder on a low-hanging rose bush.

"Dang!" I said under my breath. Chris was already at the door, ringing the bell. I came up the steps behind him.

The girls were cousins. Their self-appointed protector and guard of their honor and virginity, Bert Didier – father and uncle – was gruff with us, suspicious of our motives regarding the pretty young things in his charge, and sure we were interested only in sullying their reputations and ravaging them. The fact that he wasn't entirely wrong made his ill-tempered demeanor all the more threatening. It crossed my mind that Mr. Didier must have had a wild youth, hence his stony-eyed apprehensions where we were concerned.

"Good evening, sir," said Chris, having done this before. "We're..."

"Yeah, I know who you are. I guess... c'mon in."

We stepped inside the door, and there was an awkward pause as we all looked at each other. Just then, Mr. Didier cleared his throat and loudly called out to the girls.

"Girls, your dates are here!"

"Thank you, Mr. Didier," began Chris.

"Did I say you could talk?" More intimidation. "No, I did not. You touch a hair on the girls' heads..." looking funny at us, "...you don't bother to come in on time, which is twelve o'clock. *Twelve.*" He repeated for emphasis, just in case he hadn't intimidated us enough. He was a real piece of work.

"Twelve o'clock, yessir," said Chris.

"Did I ask you…" said Mr. Didier, "Oh, hello, girls!" He finished his sentence. It was a totally ridiculous curfew for prom night.

The girls came down the stairs. Charlotte acted as if we knew each other very well. She was swathed in lilac-colored lace. On her delicate neck was a matching satin ribbon. Her hair was piled on top of her head in a cluster of curls.

She came down the steps one at a time, walking past but not ignoring her uncle and smiling at him.

"Oh, hello, Chris," she breathed, and then turned to me, taking her corsage from my willing fingers.

"This for me?" asked Charlotte, batting her eyelashes.

I lost my ability to speak for a minute. My voice sounded funny when I said, "Yes." She smelled so good.

"Beautiful, thank you!" exclaimed Charlotte as she snapped the wristband of her corsage onto her wrist.

Christine came bounding down the stairs. She acknowledged me, then stopped in front of Chris and smiled up at him. I guess the smile that passed between them irritated her father because he bellowed about his twelve o'clock curfew again. "And don't be one minute late!" He'd had enough of all the puppy love he could handle for one evening.

We all piled into the car, Chris and Christine in front, Charlotte and I in the back. Chris peeled off in a haze of rubber-tire smoke, anxious to get the evening started and leave Didier behind.

Christine leaned over and kissed Chris' ear. "I thought we'd never get out of there!"

"Yeah!" said Chris, laughing.

"Heyyyy… Look what I got!" Charlotte pulled a joint out of her bra. She put the joint in her teeth and asked me if I had a light. The joint bobbed up and down as she spoke. Then she took one hand, put it on my knee and laughed. I looked in the rear-view mirror at my reflection, wondering where this evening would take me, and somehow realizing that things might never be the same again.

There was a marvelous kind of excitement as we pulled up to the school. Everyone was filled with anticipation. There were shiny limos with girls alighting in dresses of every hue, with their tuxedoed escorts. There was perfume, aftershave, and wildly surging hormones in the air.

At the entrance, Mr. Jacob, the principal, was taking the prom tickets. "Evening, ladies and gentlemen! Don't forget the code of conduct you were given in assembly last week." Few had any intention whatsoever of heeding his warning.

Everyone oohed as they entered. The decorating committee had done a fabulous job of transforming our gym into a 1920s speakeasy. I think the theme was appropriate considering how many students had managed to surreptitiously bring alcohol to the prom, right under the ostensibly watchful eyes of the faculty and administration. This includes my brother, who had brought a flask for the occasion and filled it with the rarely-touched vodka from our home. There was such a mélange of color, music, laughter, moving bodies, twinkling lights, and cleavage, I found my excitement fused with the sex-besotted youthful joy of it all. All my senses were on high alert to the swirling blues and greens and various tints, the sounds, the overheated breathlessness of frenetic young people blowing off a lot of pent-up steam. It seemed to a lowly sophomore like me almost impossibly glamorous and sophisticated.

All our friends were there. In their rented tuxedos, they looked older to me. I thought I could catch a glimpse of the men they would become. After the first few dances, I found Chris and Tim lingering by one of the huge, cut-glass punch bowls that had been donated by someone's parents for the occasion. They reflected the light with the ruby punch casting a red glow on the table.

Our dates had gone to the ladies' room en masse – just something girls seemed to do. If one went, they all went. Tim was about to lift his punch glass to his mouth when Chris stopped him.

"Hold on a minute, partner." Chris turned his back to the crowd. He pulled his flask from inside his boot and poured some alcohol into Tim's punch glass. "This'll put hair on your chest."

Tim knocked back the punch. Then Chris, who had been spiking the punch for the last twenty minutes, poured a little bit more into the punch bowl. I came by just at that moment and took a big, long swig.

"Somebody spiked the punch!" I laughed and put my arm around Tim's shoulder. I was feeling more and more loose and relaxed. I liked being part of this celebration of everything young and beautiful... And I definitely liked Charlotte's low-cut dress that made me feel very, very grateful to my brother for convincing my father and mother to let me be part of all this.

"ALL RIGHT, LADIES AND GENTS! IT'S NOW TIME FOR THE SOULLLLLLL TRAIN DANCE-OFF!!!" said the DJ over the loudspeaker. He put on "Love Machine!" The crowd drew two lines, and each solo dancer prepared to dance down the center of the line, like on the television show "Soul Train".

Tim, being a naturally good dancer, went first. He looked pretty damn good popping and locking down the dance floor.

"Me next!" Chris called it, doing the robot down the line.

I downed my entire glass of spiked punch, wiped my mouth, and said.

"Okay. I'm in." Chris started laughing at the end of the Soul Train dance line because he'd never seen me dance in his life. "Watch. And. Learn." I said, as I did a perfectly executed long slide onto the dance floor.

The assembled crowd approved, which emboldened me. The almost primitive beat of the bass coming up through the floor made me feel like electricity was running through my veins. I could feel it in my whole body. That, and my brother's vodka most definitely lowered my inhibitions.

I started doing the hustle down the line. Little did anyone know that I'd been secretly practicing to *Saturday Night Fever*'s hit album all year, and I was ready for my moment in the sun.

"Wow!" Tim was impressed and whooped his approval.

"What the???" My brother's mouth was agape. I don't think until that moment he thought his baby brother had one scintilla of coolness.

Rhonda, the hot African-American head cheerleader, jumped up and did the bump with me all the way to the end of the line. Then she curtsied to me, and in return, I did a split and pulled myself back up by my suit collar.

"What the hell?!?" Chris was laughing and shouting. The crowd went wild, and everyone started cheering and clapping. The timing was absolute perfection because as I was dancing, feeding on the cheers and clapping, that's when all the girls returned from the ladies' room and caught my exuberant, alcohol-lubricated act.

"Wow!" Charlotte raised her eyebrows at me.

Everyone had compliments and cheers for me. Truthfully, I was feeling pretty proud of myself, bolstered by the praise of the crowd. My moment in the sun gave me confidence, making me less tentative and more assured with Charlotte. Damn, I felt good. Slow-dancing with Charlotte, with the creamy white skin of her cleavage pressed against me, was the best feeling I'd had in my life.

A few hours of happiness went by like this. But all too soon, it was time for the girls to go home. They seemed to be the only girls with a curfew like this.

Chris pulled me aside. "Dude, dude, we gotta go. It's 11:30 P.M."

I was having too much fun dancing with Charlotte, Rhonda, and some upperclassmen whose names I didn't know. "No, man, I'm having a good time. Leave me alone." I laughed.

"Okay, dude. It's your funeral," Chris told me seriously.

Somehow he managed to wrangle us together to his car. We were all feeling no pain at all, and Chris must have felt like he was wrangling cats, but with some effort he got us on the road and the end of what seemed to me a perfect night. I was having the time of my life, and I resented it ending all too fast.

But in the back of the car, Charlotte was making our departure easier.

Chris turned up the radio full blast when Boston's "More Than a Feeling" came on. "All right, man, I love this song!" He sang along – badly – as did Christine. But there was a kind of jubilation in their singing that somehow made the flat notes and off-key warbling seem just right.

Charlotte, sequestered over in her corner, started giggling a little and twirling her hair. I looked over at her for a long moment.

"Take a picture, it'll last longer." She half-smiled and scooted across the seat next to mine. Whispering in my ear, she put one hand on my thigh, softly biting my earlobe. Until that moment, I had no idea the ear was an erogenous zone. I couldn't help myself. Both my feet jammed into the floorboard as she stuck her tongue in my ear. "Damnnnnn…" I said softly under my breath.

Charlotte pulled back for a minute to see what I was thinking.

I put my forehead to hers, then softly, slowly, I took a sip of her bottom, half-curled lip. As I pressed forward, stealing yet another kiss, and another from her, Charlotte shuddered with pleasure.

We made out for several minutes. Chris and Christine were preoccupied with their inebriated, discordant songfest and took no notice of us. In the back seat, Charlotte and I were steaming up the windows.

When he pulled up in front of Didier's house, my brother finally turned around. "Do I have to get a hose to separate you two?" He was laughing. "We're here. C'mon, man, we gotta get the girls inside."

As Charlotte and I slowly disentangled, all she said was, "Wow… just wow." That single syllable word made me feel pretty good.

Didier, holding his shotgun at his side, was as gruff and inhospitable as he had been when we picked up our dates; and hovered as we said our good-nights awkwardly in front of him, rushing our dates inside. I had no idea if I would ever see Charlotte again as I turned and walked back to the car, feeling both elated by the evening I had just had and sullen and aggrieved by its abrupt ending.

How do I describe the rest of that night? It's part farce, part fear, part something out of a John Hughes movie, and part complete and utter magic – a night I will never forget.

"That guy's crazy!" Chris said as we got in the car.

"Yeah, man. Nuts. Whoa. Who actually comes to the door with a shotgun? That's like a cliché from Depression-Era Appalachia. Dad would be furious if he knew he threatened us with a gun."

"Yeah, well, don't tell him," my brother answered me with a wicked grin.

He drove around the block in the alley behind the girls' house, then pulled the car over. He looked around a bit as if to check for witnesses. I had no idea what we were doing there.

He told me he had a surprise for me, and I suddenly felt very wary. I had a feeling he was going do something very risky, and I was part of his plan.

"Let me put it to you this way... the night isn't over, yet." Chris told me this in a deliberately mysterious fashion. He got out of the car and opened the trunk, pulled out two brown paper grocery store bags, and threw one bag at me.

I just gave him a look. He told me that my big brother had plans and pointed to his head. I opened the bag and found a pair of my sneakers and jogging clothes.

"We're going jogging at this time of night?"

"Yeah, right," said Chris. There we were, in the middle of Didier's suburban neighborhood, his white BVDs glaring in the light of the street lamp.

I asked him if he was drunk or high, or both. He just told me he had everything under control, to trust him and follow his lead, and I would definitely *not* be sorry. I was doubtful, but younger brother that I was, I followed. Following meant changing my clothes right there in the alley, and a whole lot more.

He was looking up at Christine's window, so I looked up, too. The lights went on and off twice, obviously some kind of signal, and Chris's master plan became very clear to me. "Are you crazy? I really don't want to die tonight!"

He just told me that not only was I not going to die tonight, I was going to really *live* tonight. "Now up and over." He gestured to the California, baby-puke pink, six-foot-high wall that separated the alley from the Didier house. "And be quiet."

We do the craziest things when we're young, and I must have been crazy because I followed him, even with Didier's shotgun fresh in my mind and fear in the pit of my stomach. We scaled the wall; and sneaked through the foliage to the back of the house, where the Didiers had a little sunroom and an old porch that was now a gardening room for Didier's wife. Like two Romeos or Casanovas or Don Juans, or simply two sex-starved adolescents, we climbed the grapevine-covered lattice to the window of our two Juliets.

Christine grinned as she hung out the window, watching us climb.

I looked up at her. She turned around and whispered, "Hey Char, look what I found." Then Charlotte was at the window, the moonlight washing across her face just so, making her look so lovely, my fear became less and my motivation to get up that trellis was enhanced tenfold.

I was not as accustomed to these undercover operations as my brother apparently was. I carefully climbed the lattice work, then hoisted myself up onto the roof of the sunroom.

Charlotte reached out for me. I pulled myself halfway into the window. Charlotte gave me a little kiss, then she helped me through.

I felt as though I had crossed into another universe. I had never been in a girl's bedroom before. I was suddenly surrounded by frills and ruffles, lace and ribbons, keepsakes, heart-shaped boxes, dried flowers, perfume, and a pink feather boa draped across a mirror. There were twin beds with floral chintz spreads. It seemed almost impossibly feminine, and made me feel all the more masculine in contrast. It was a secret chamber, an enigmatic fortress of femininity to which I had heretofore not been admitted, and now I had been given access to something clandestine and mysterious. The effect was enhanced by Christine having lit scented candles all around the room. A record was playing ever so softly. She and Chris were already in the thick of things on her bed.

Still, I was cautious. "Won't your uncle hear us?" I said, nervously looking around as Charlotte wrapped her arms around my waist. She assured me that "Uncle Pete" was already passed out in the basement, the victim of too many Budweisers. He won't come out of hibernation until the morning.

"Really?" I said.

"Really," she said, putting her arms around my neck and kissing me. It was then that I threw all caution to the wind.

I melted into her embrace. The chemistry between us was so instantaneous, so incendiary, that within moments, we were naked. As I looked down at her, I thought she was the most beautiful thing I had ever seen in my entire life, and I told her so. She trembled as I stroked her perfect baby-smooth skin that felt so hot to my touch. Charlotte melted underneath my next embrace. We were transported to a world of our own.

"I've never..." confessed Charlotte.

"Me, either..." I confessed. "I would never do anything to hurt you. I promise."

She said, "I know."

Outside, it had suddenly begun to pour, and the rhythm of the rain beat against the tin roof of the sunroom.

A faint rumbling woke me first. I was disoriented and didn't know what it was. Then somehow, I just knew it was the sound of a trash can being rolled out for pick-up. My muddled brain sent me an urgent message: "Danger! Danger! Didier must be up. Oh! My! God!"

I looked over at beautiful Charlotte, and I realized that:

a.) my other hand was underneath her body;
b.) that my whole arm was dead asleep from lack of circulation;
c.) that I was completely naked;
d.) that Charlotte was completely naked; and
e.) what was worse, the man with the shotgun was awake.

And not only was he awake, but he was up and mobile outside, in the alleyway that was our only means of escape.

I jumped out of bed faster than if someone had called, "Fire!" I desperately searched for my clothes and put them on, hopping on one leg.

"Get up! Get up! Get the hell up!" I whispered to my brother, who was also naked. Christine was also naked. I did the math: four naked people and Didier's gun = dead. Dead, deader, deadest. I shook my brother awake with my good hand.

"Get up, Chris!"

Then he too had that same heart-stopping realization.

"Jesus H. Christ!" He sprang out of bed, throwing off the sheet.

"Hey!" Christine was now naked to me. She covered her breasts with one arm and her privates with her other hand.

"Your father is up, and we are all *muerto*!!!" Chris whispered.

"Oh my God, he'll kill us!" Christine was horrified.

"Sshhhhhh! For the love of all that is holy, shhhhh!" Chris begged her.

Charlotte looked absolutely stricken, but was silent, her eyes darting all around the room.

Somehow, we were dressed in Guinness Book of World Records time; and Chris furtively checked our only escape route, looking through the window to the yard below to see if there was any way to avoid a terrible fate that could await us if we encountered the monstrous Didier. Could we possibly go out the way we two bold Lotharios had come in?

Didier, who had heard Christine cry out, yelled, "Girls! Everything all right upstairs?" We knew he'd grab that damn shotgun even before we heard him thundering up the stairs. Christine jumped up, threw on her nightie, and locked the bedroom door. By now, Charlotte was so terrified, she was shaking; but she managed to throw on an oversized t-shirt.

"Go, go, go, go, go, go, *go*!!!" Christine was practically shoving us out the window. My heart was beating so hard and so fast, I could hear it like a kettle drum pounding in my ears like a death knell.

"Girls!" Didier, that psychopathic killer of teenage boys, was at the door. He tried the knob. "Why is this door locked?"

The girls were trembling, so terrified that they had lost their ability to speak.

"Goddammit, open this door right now!"

Somehow, Christine found her voice. "I didn't mean to lock it. Wait a sec, we're getting dressed." The words came out, but they sounded thin and shaky.

My sweatsuit snagged on the window latch.

"Get out before he kicks the door in!" Christine was almost in tears.

Chris told Christine to hold Didier off for as long as possible, and followed me out the window.

"Do I hear male voices in there?" He banged on the door. No answer. He banged on the door again. "I'm going to kill those little bastards!" I could hear him yelling as I was climbing down the rickety trellis.

We were running for our lives, and had already rounded the corner of the alley and were almost to the car when Chris, in a panic, thought he'd lost his keys. He was so rattled, he didn't even realize he was holding them in his hand, the hand that was shaking so much he could barely unlock the door.

I turned and saw Didier now in the yard, head looming over the top of the six-foot wall. He must have been standing on something. He was too fat to get his heft up and over, but he could pull himself up high enough with one arm that his face could be seen. He was apoplectic.

"You little pricks!" He was cocking his shotgun. I think the crazy SOB was actually going to shoot us. Chris and I rounded the corner of Didier's street, burning rubber.

I was totally freaked out and very angry. I punched Chris on his arm as hard as I could. "You almost got us killed!"

"Are you kidding? I think what you really mean to say is, 'Thank you, Chris, for the best night of my pathetic little life.'" My brother had somehow gone from being terrified to cool in a nanosecond.

"You are an asshole," I said. "You know that?" I turned my face to the window. I was damned if I was going to talk to him the rest of the way home. But maybe he was right; I had my brother to thank for one of the most memorable, magical nights of my young life.

When we got back to our house, Chris put the rest of his plan in motion. Knowing it was possible that our father would be up, he told me to just do as he said. I wasn't really in the mood to listen to his crap any more of his schemes, but I resentfully let him talk because I had no plan at all. I just glared at him.

"Listen, Michael, listen to me. Dad may be outside, so just go along and we'll be OK." The plan was we were to jog up to the house as though we'd gotten up early and gone for a run. When I said dad would ask where Chris's car was, Chris would just say we wanted to come home in Tim's limo, and we were going to jog over to school and pick up the car after breakfast. The whole thing seemed preposterous, and I was truly amazed at my brother's talent for deception. He had told a massive string of lies for the past twenty-four hours. It seemed to come to him so easily.

But damn, it seemed to work as we jogged up to the house and greeted my father, who was out front watering the roses. We had our breakfast while my mother asked us numerous questions about the prom, and my father seemed none the wiser. As I sat eating pancakes and bacon, I thought, grudgingly, "My brother is an evil genius."

Only with the benefit of time can I see that it was after his senior year that my brother began to lose his way. There are so many choices we make in this life, and we don't understand when we're young that they can affect everything that comes after. Chris and my father had had major arguments; and my mother and Chris, quiet talks because Chris wanted to take a year off before starting college. His grades and SAT scores were good enough to get into a fairly good school, but he had adamantly refused to apply anywhere. I think Chris thought he was going to go off backpacking through Europe. He had some money he'd saved up, but not enough. And my father, just as adamantly as Chris, refused to subsidize his travels. With a finality that was unusual for him, he told Chris that if he wasn't going to go to college, he had to work.

I don't know. Maybe dad should have let him go. It might have been good for my brother, but that's not the way things played out.

Looking in the bathroom mirror, Chris combed his hair back carefully, then sprayed it with a cloud of Adorn hairspray. My brother was a really good-looking guy and he had a lot of style – even if it worked better some times than others – he always seemed to have panache.

I watched him as he dressed in a nylon disco shirt that was festooned with the image of a flying unicorn across the right pec in bronze and white. He was wearing Jordache Flared Bell-Bottom jeans and a gold metal disco belt. He had on two-inch white platform shoes. To top it off, he was wearing a white puka-shell necklace. I thought it was more of a costume than anything else, and I laughed at his get-up. He just told me I had no sense of fashion and that I was too conventional, and didn't have the imagination he had. He put on some Chapstick and some Hai Karate aftershave, checked out his disco look, then nodded at his reflection in the mirror. He was satisfied.

When he came downstairs, my father asked "Prince Charming" where he was off to. My brother told him he was off to the mall.

"Oh! Great! Job hunting?" my father said. He knew full well that wasn't my brother's intent, but Chris dissembled quickly and said that's what he had in mind.

"Great, go fill out applications, try for ten today." My father looked him up and down. "But Chris, you cannot go dressed like... like... this... Elvis, or whatever."

I guess I must have laughed because they both shot me a look that said I, in no uncertain terms, should stay out of this. But my brother turned and went upstairs without a word. When he came down, he was dressed more conservatively. It wasn't him, and I think that was part of the problem.

As he was walking out the door, I saw my mother press some money into his hand and whisper, "This is for lunch. Don't tell your dad." She didn't ordinarily keep things from my father. But every once in a while, when she wanted to indulge us a little, it was *entre nous*. I think indulging us was my mother's secret vice.

I think he honestly tried, walking up and down both floors of the mall, stopping everywhere. But he was either told there were no openings or he was simply handed an application to fill out, like any number of other job applicants at the various establishments he tried. Things had always come easily to Chris, and a day of rejection was something he'd never experienced. I'm not sure what he expected, maybe that his charm and good looks would land him any job he wanted, that things would continue to come as easily as they always had. He had wanted a year off to figure out what he wanted to do with his life, to figure out where he fit in the scheme of things, to have no pressure and lots of time. But dad had laid down the law, and he found himself brought up short by reality.

I guess the dejection he felt was evident because, as he sat down to think where he might go next, he heard someone say, "Looking for a job, son?"

He looked up to see an officer sitting at a table outside the US Army recruitment office. The officer introduced himself as Sergeant Jakes. "Or maybe a career? This is a great place to start, son." He gave my brother a pretty good pitch about the military being not just a job, but a career; that he would be respected; and that family and friends would look at him differently. He gave Chris an application to take home. "I'm always here. Come back and see me and we can talk."

Jakes was the only person who gave Chris a green light to a future, though the military was never what he had in mind. But Jakes was so friendly and encouraging, Chris took the application home. They shook hands. Jakes' grip was like a vice, but the quarterback in Chris let him meet Jakes with equal force. Jakes liked that, and he smiled. "You're definitely Army material, son."

After dinner, Chris told dad about his problems turning in applications, and the reactions he was getting from employers with him not having any work experience. Together, they sat down at the kitchen table and worked on his applications to the various businesses where he was trying to get employment.

Dad reminded Chris, "Wait a minute, it's not true you have no work history. You've got experience. You and your brother ran your own lawn-mowing service every summer from junior high throughout high school, keeping all the little old ladies' lawns trim and neat in the neighborhood. That's entrepreneurship, son, terrific experience. And you were also the class president in your junior and senior year of high school, running the student council. You forgot about that. That's leadership, son. Don't you realize that? And your quarterback role was leadership."

The Army brochure was in the stack of applications. Dad picked it up, with Sergeant Jakes' card stapled at the top. "Who's Jakes?" he asked.

My brother told him he was just some guy at the mall who tried to recruit him. I knew my father was dubious. He just wanted Chris to get an entry-level job, see how tedious it was, and apply to colleges for the spring semester. But he did try to help Chris. "And don't forget, all your customers can give excellent recommendations to all these places you're applying to. You coached kids' basketball classes on Thursday nights at the Y, and you volunteered summers all through high school. That shows you're civic-minded." My brother had always been such an operator, I was surprised he hadn't thought of that himself. I think that was because his heart wasn't in it. But what I think he did like was that in conversing with my father about all this, he got to see that dad respected the things he had done, and that alone lifted his spirits. It was a gift my father didn't even realize he'd given Chris.

Chris got to the mall when it opened. He went to each store he had applied to, and asked for the manager. It took hours to go from store to store, but he got them all turned in. He got a couple of mini-interviews because this time, he was armed with our father's respect. When he was asked if he had any work experience, he was able to say with some pride, "I do. I didn't work for anyone, but I ran my own lawn-mowing service every spring and summer with my brother, all four years of high school, and I have excellent references." The responses were positive.

His last application was at Tuesday's. He was tired by the time he got there. He'd been inside a mall all day, working on getting a job he didn't even really want. But after last night's talk, he did want to please my father. The good responses he was getting served to keep him making a real effort. When he stepped into the restaurant, it was dark. They were open, but their staff was light. They were between shifts. He waited for several minutes and was just about to leave when a busboy came by.

"Excuse me, may I see the manager, please?"

The busboy signaled, "Just a moment."

He waited again, and was just beginning to get annoyed when the lights of the restaurant were turned on. Walking toward him was the most beautiful redhead he had ever seen in his life, dressed all in black, with a black waiter's apron tied around her wasp-like waist. She sized him up and down.

"You asked for a manager?" she asked, with her sexy Boston accent.

He was stunned by her outright, stone-cold foxiness. For a moment, he was at a loss for words, definitely not something that happened often to my loquacious brother.

"Yeah, what do you want?" she asked, thinking he was there trying to sell her something.

He recovered his game. "I want a job. Got one?"

"Why didn't you say so?" She was a bit more friendly now. "Come to the bar." She stood behind the bar, and he took a stool. She put her reading glasses on the tip of her nose and looked down at his application. Somehow, the glasses made her even more appealing.

"Quarterback, huh?" she grinned over her glasses.

"Yes, and I had my own lawn-mowing…" Chris started.

"I can read," she said with a half-grin. "Look, kid," The "kid" rankled Chris. "I just fired a guy last night for breaking a bunch of glasses. Since you were a quarterback, I can assume you're coordinated. So, look, we're short-staffed. I need someone to start tonight, dinner shift. You'd just be shadowing the busboys to start. Later in the week, more serious training. Can you start tonight?"

It all seemed to happen so fast. And this woman was so gorgeous, my brother didn't hesitate, nor did he stop to think. He just said yes and started at three that very afternoon.

Chris didn't give a thought to any of the other applications he'd dropped off. If he was going to get to work with this beautiful sexy creature every day, this stunner who everyone called Ginger because of her gorgeous red tresses, that sealed the deal for him and assuaged some of the resentment he felt about not backpacking through Europe. My brother would always be swayed by a beautiful face, a curvaceous body, and a perfect ass.

I was home when he returned. I heard him say, "Hey, mom. I am now officially among the employed." He seemed happy as he threw his keys on the small table by the front door. Of course, my mother hugged him. Mom hugged us every chance she could. She was always affectionate, encouraging and loving. He called my father at work, who was pleased and gave him lots of "Attaboys".

It was true my brother had experience working for himself, but he'd never had a job before with corporate rules, paperwork to fill out, and a boss looking over his shoulder. Reporting for work he saw Ginger's titian mane glowing beneath the overhead lights of the bar like a beacon. Goddamn, he was a pushover for a beautiful woman; and this one was a veritable siren. He stood there for a moment.

"Take a picture. It'll last longer."

Chris was only slightly embarrassed he'd been caught staring at her.

"Follow me, Quarterback. You've got paperwork to fill out." That was what she called him from then on.

He trained under a guy named Nixon… yes, Nixon. Chris was a smart guy, and sports had taught him to follow intricate plays, so he caught on fast, even to Ginger's plays. It was evident to him that when she wasn't being a hard-nosed boss, she was most definitely flirtatious and suggestive with him. What he hadn't quite figured out yet was what she wanted from him besides work, if anything. Was she just a natural flirt, or did she want to take this somewhere? He figured since he was the employee and she the boss, the next move was up to her.

But he did know he liked getting a paycheck, and he figured that by the end of the summer, he really could do his backpacking thing.

Though the work was tedious and offered no stimulation, Chris did work hard. Ginger continued to half-flirt with him, half-mock him with the Quarterback label, at the same time being the tough, no-nonsense taskmaster. Chris just kept waiting and watching, uncertain what to make of her.

After a few weeks, late one night when they were closing up, she asked him if he was tired. She'd never been the least solicitous of him before, but he was almost too exhausted to notice. He just nodded. She invited him into her office to sit down. Chris flopped into a chair and exhaled long and slow.

"Nice work, Quarterback. You catch on fast." She leaned forward and slapped him on the knee, and then rubbed it a little. Chris tried to be nonchalant, but as tired as he was, he was definitely turned on. He was, after all, a young and healthy guy; and this wasn't just any average female. This was Ginger.

But then she confused him again, going from sultry to all business. As she finished tallying up the night's takings, she talked to him, giving him little training tidbits as she went along. "As you get used to the Tuesday's way of serving the customer," she told Chris, "after you've mastered the art of being a busboy, that is," she said with a wink, "you'll start shadowing someone on the wait staff. That means you'll follow them for a few days. You'll see them take an order, place the order the kitchen, and serve the table. This is the way you'll learn to be a waiter. No tips. But you'll learn the ins and outs of being a Tuesday's employee."

"Okay," said Chris, exhausted. What went thought his mind was, "Does she think I really care about this, about being a freaking waiter? I'm outta here as soon as I have enough money."

But then she said something that got his attention again.

"Hey, but tonight, you'll get a little tip, later."

He thought that was undeniably suggestive. She was fucking with him like he was some uninitiated rube.

She told him she'd be done shortly, and went over the numbers one last time with her calculator. "Phew! I balanced the drawer. Thank God. You have no idea what a hassle it is if you're just one penny off. Restaurant work is no joke."

"You're telling me," he said to himself as he rubbed his aching neck.

"Aw, I'll make it up to you later. I'll buy you a beer sometime. Hey, walk me to the car in a minute?"

"Sure." That sounded encouraging. He hadn't ever seen anyone else walk her to her car. She finished all her closing duties, untied her apron, folded it up, grabbed her purse, spritzed herself with a little perfume, and said, "Let's go!"

Chris stood, not without a little difficulty, and stretched out his back as he felt like an old man.

"Rough night?" she put her hand on his shoulder, then rubbed it a little. "I know how it feels. I did every job in this place other than dishwasher before I became manager. You'll get used to it."

Chris didn't really want to get used to it. What he wanted was to travel. But he straightened up, his shoulders automatically tightening. He instinctively bulked up when she touched him, letting her feel his muscles, which truly were impressive.

"Walk me to the car," she said, opening the door.

She flipped off the restaurant lights, and checked all the front locks. They were walking out the back door when she flipped on the alarm system. As they stepped out into the cool night air, Ginger turned and locked up Tuesday's for the night. Chris stretched his back again. She turned to him and smiled.

"I'm over here," she said, pointing to one of the few cars still left in the lot.

"Very cool," he said, admiring her cherry red Firebird. "Nice T-tops."

"Thanks," she said. "I worked hard for it. Where are you?"

"I'm over there." He pointed to his car a few spaces away. "That's me," he said.

"Nice Camaro. I always liked them. Let me see inside." He unlocked the passenger door and she slipped inside. He got inside and shut the door.

"Let's hear her sound," she said. He started the engine.

"Impressive, but I meant the stereo." She grinned.

"It's really fine," he told her, cranking up the sound. She played with him, toyed with him and teased him. And just when he was about as turned on as possible, she got out of the car, shut the door and said good night, smiling and knowing exactly what she was doing. She was the ultimate queen and he was goddamn angry about being played like a violin. But that didn't put an end to his total infatuation.

Chris worked, learned, and got good at everything Ginger threw at him. One night, when he was clocking out and taking off his apron, about to walk out the door, Ginger stopped him.

"Wait a minute, Quarterback. Here are your tips." She handed him ten dollars in ones. She looked up at him with her green eyes through a fringe of heavily mascaraed lashes and said, "I work a double today. You doing anything this evening? I'll be off at ten o'clock. Pick me up by my car."

He told her he was surprised, but absolutely up for whatever she had in mind.

The rest, I would never have known if he hadn't told me one night when he'd had God knows how many shots of vodka. After he had drunkenly called Ginger a cock tease and a bitch and several other choice adjectives, he began to talk. What he said was circuitous in the manner of the deeply, thoroughly inebriated; but from what I could piece together, it went something like this.

After making him crazy for weeks on end, nicknaming him Quarterback, giving him significant looks and brushing up against him whenever no one was looking, she told him to meet her at the mall parking lot a little after ten. I guess around ten-thirty, he got tired of sitting, and got out of the car to stretch his legs. He was perched on the hood of his car when she got out of the restaurant and met him at the parking lot.

"Good. You're on time," she said.

"Good evening, to you, too, beautiful," he said, opening his door.

"Oh, no. My car this time. Get in." She gunned the motor and drove off fast.

He is been dated, always the one desired, the one who made the decisions about whether or not things would move forward. With Ginger, he felt off balance, unsure. It was a feeling he didn't like, and it made him simmer with anger at her, but that just added to the attraction. For sure, it wasn't healthy, but he couldn't resist. She reached down and squeezed his thigh, just above the knee. He was turned on as he always was with her. He really had a thing for her. She exited Laurel Canyon, and headed up the mountain.

"Where are we going?" he asked.

She told him he'd know when they get there. She was in command. Keeping her eyes on the road, she pulled into the deep curves on Mulholland Drive, the road that snaked its way perilously atop the Santa Monica mountain range, separating the Valley from the city side of LA. He was wary as she clipped along at a pace that was too fast for the hairpin curves. It put him on edge but somehow turned him on, all the more as he looked to the side of the road, where the lack of guardrails made things dangerous. "Just like Ginger," he thought – dangerous. They followed the curves of the road, and then finally stopped at an overlook just before Woodrow Wilson Drive that had a spectacular view of the entire valley.

"Here we are," she said when she'd parked.

"You've been here before, huh?" She didn't answer as she walked in front of the car's headlights, stood dead in the middle, looked at him, and stripped off her top. There she was, standing with all that pale flesh glowing in the headlights, her cleavage demarcated only by the lace on her black bra. He wanted her like he'd never wanted any of his high school flames. This was a whole other league.

She walked around to the passenger side of the car and commanded him to get out in the tone of a dominatrix or what he imagined one would sound like. She untucked his T-shirt from his jeans. She then took the bottom of the shirt, and ripped it wide open, bottom-to-top. It was an aggressive move that made him wildly turned on. "Get in the back seat, Quarterback."

Chris was ready to go with whatever she wanted. But first, he reached forward to kiss her. She allowed it, though he could tell it wasn't her thing. She flipped open both T-tops and took them off, flipped the top of bucket seat forward and reached down, pushing the bucket seat forward as far as it would go. "Get in."

Chris slipped into the back seat. He was blindingly crazy with desire. Ginger stood inside the driver's side door, slipped down her black work slacks, kicked them off, and stood there in her black bikini panties and black lacy bra. He took time to just breathe in the image.

"What are you waiting for, man? Christmas?" she said, poking her head inside the car. He struggled with his belt. "It's a lot easier if you just do what I did. Do it now!"

He struggled to get out of the back seat. He pulled down his jeans and hopped around in his white BVDs, trying to get the skinny legged jeans off his feet. After he'd managed to unburden himself of his clothes, he reached over to turn off the headlights.

"I want 'em on," she told him, wrapping her arms around his neck and pulling him on top of her. She began kissing his neck. Ginger got on top of him, straddling him like she was riding on a saddle. "You gotta work on your moves, Quarterback." she said, intimating that he wasn't very seductive. "And those tighty-whities, man," she laughed a little. "They gotta go. Seriously."

He flipped her off of him onto the other side of the car. He stripped off his underwear and got on top of her. "They're gone," he said. Chris pinned Ginger to the seat, reached down, pulled down her panties, separated her legs, and penetrated her. She'd worked him into such a frenzy the sex was short and urgent, and Ginger was immobilized.

"That was incredible," Chris breathed. But, Ginger was silent. I guess it was incredible to him, but to her, not so much.

She popped open the driver's side door, and extricated herself from the back seat. "Yeah," she said, matter-of-factly, "it was alright." She stood up and pulled up her panties. He hadn't even undone her bra. He realized he'd been much too fast. He pulled himself out of the car and hopped around, putting on his underwear and jeans.

"Listen, listen," he said, "we can... Can we go again?" She had made him feel inadequate now. She found her clothes, which were strewn about the car, and got dressed.

Just as they were putting on their shirts, a patrol car pulled up and slowed down.

"Everything okay here?" asked the cop. He could probably guess that they had just been necking, at the *very* least.

Chris said his heart pounded in his chest. But she just coolly put her arm around Chris' neck, and said, "Just enjoying the beautiful view, officer," smiling flirtatiously.

"Okay, ma'am, you have a good night," he said, smiling back at the beautiful redhead.

Ginger got in the car and started the engine. She slammed her door shut, lit a joint, and told him to get in the car. There was no warmth in her voice. She sat silently, looking forward at the road, smoking her blunt without even a glance at him.

Chris got dressed. The afterglow of sex had already worn off, being crushed by her less than enthusiastic response to his technique and the untimely intrusion of the police officer. He got in, fastened his seat belt, and Ginger took off, cruising down the curvy, mountainous, midnight road, one hand on the wheel, one hand holding her joint.

She pulled up to his car, silently reached across him to his door handle, and opened it.

"Ginger, listen, if you just…" he started to say, but Ginger wasn't interested in listening.

"Just get out. I'm tired, and I have a big day tomorrow." She never gave him a chance after that to be anything but boss and employee. She was cool and aloof, never called him Quarterback again. She just dropped him, never looked at him or spoke to him unless it was absolutely necessary. It left him dejected, his confidence flagging. Then she fired him on the spot the day he was bussing a table and had dishes in one hand and a half-finished pitcher of beer in the other, when a woman at one of the tables abruptly rose to go to the ladies' room and crashed into Chris. She got splashed with beer, ruining her expensive silk blouse.

That was also the day that my brother, with beer and food all over his clothes, found Sergeant Jakes, walked up to him and asked, "Where do I sign?"

Chapter 3

Malibu

P ATRICK'S WAS JAMMED as usual. Larry pulled up in front and dropped off his wife, Pam, off to stand in line while he looked for a parking space. Ricky had already parked and joined his mother in the line as they waited. It was cold at the beach in February. Maybe not a northeasterner's idea of cold, but definitely cold for southern Californians.

The hostess greeted Ricky by name. As they were being seated at a table in the sun, as Pam had requested, Larry joined them. Solicitous as always, he rubbed his wife's arm asked if she was warm enough. They ordered coffee all around, then had their usual back-and-forth about what to order. They probably knew the menu by heart, but that didn't preclude their discussion.

They were a happy family. Were all happy families alike, as Tolstoy had said? Perhaps. This one bantered and teased and bickered with good cheer and affection. Ricky was an only child; and as such, he had received all their love and attention. But they hadn't spoiled him.

"Gorgeous day," Ricky said as he looked out the window. He loved Malibu. This was exactly where he wanted to spend the rest of his life. He had absolutely no doubt whatsoever that he could and would make that happen. He felt young, strong and healthy; and he knew what he wanted. The whole family was in real estate, but Ricky wasn't interested in LA. It was only Malibu where he felt he had a future.

Larry looked at his son. "At least let us put the land in the family trust. It will be protection if things don't turn out the way you'd like." Ricky countered that things were going to go just fine. But to quell his father's concern, he conceded.

"But honey, the rents are so high in Malibu."

"I won't be renting long. I'm going to build here."

Both parents looked dubious and concerned. This was a continuation of an ongoing conversation they'd had for some time, with Ricky's parents trying to make him see how impractical his plans were. He shouldn't limit himself to Malibu real estate because he was narrowing his potential of properties. Ricky countered with the assurance of youth that he knew where his passions lay and he could do this. He felt it in his gut.

His father conceded that it was a miracle that he'd gotten the land he'd purchased for such a steal. "So, when do you think you're going to be able to build this dream house you're always raving about?"

"It'll take me a few years. Besides, I'm not even dating anyone seriously now. There's no bride waiting in the wings. I don't feel pressure to rush."

While they didn't necessarily agree, they were a family full of genuine warmth and affection for one another, and each of them knew this. After they had finished their breakfast and hugged one another goodbye, Ricky's parents reminded him that they would be in San Francisco for a few weeks, and they needed him to look after their Westwood properties.

As Ricky pulled out of Patrick's onto Entrada Drive, he rolled the top down on his Stingray Corvette convertible. As he waited for the light to turn at the Pacific Coast Highway, he looked at the glittering ocean before him and sighed. A sailboat made its way slowly across the horizon, and he put on his sunglasses. He thought about his future and the sweet home he was going to put on his property once he put the money together to build it. He had no doubt money would come. He was going to make it so.

"Come hell or high water," Ricky said to himself.

He'd known for some time that this was where he wanted to spend his life. As he drove up the PCH and looked at the glittering ocean and swaying palms, the long fronds shivery and silver with sunlight and passing cars with surfboards and kayaks, he felt surer than ever.

When he pulled into his gravel driveway, the only construction on the lot, he thought with supreme confidence that the money would happen, the house would happen, a wife would happen. It would all happen because he would make it so. There was not a shadow of doubt in this mind; and he smiled, a happy young man contemplating his future.

His lot was ocean-adjacent, but in Malibu, he had the main thing: a view. The view had a future because nothing could structurally be built in front of it due to fear of landslides. He got out of his car and walked to the center of the lot, master of all he surveyed.

"Honey, I'm home!" he said quietly under his breath and smiled.

After checking his property, Ricky went into the office for a few hours to do some paperwork and make some phone calls. When he was done showing a few properties, it was already late afternoon. He grabbed a couple of quick tacos at the local stand and decided to go out for a few drinks, just to finish off a perfect Friday. He figured a couple of his friends would be there. It would be fun.

When Ricky arrived at the Crazy Fox, the place was already filled with the energy of the crowd. He could feel the bass coming up through the floor as the music blasted. He threaded his way through the packed, undulating dance floor to his friend TJ the DJ. He gave TJ some good-natured ribbing about the music he was playing: his least favorite, disco. He had a life, friends, parents who loved him, goals, and a plucky, bold, self-assurance, a sense of humor, and every reason to enjoy the moment. Nothing had ever really been more than he could handle. As the saying goes, "God's in his heaven and all's right with the world."

He bantered with his friends and played a little pool, winning some of the games while his friends groaned. There was an unarticulated consensus among his posse that Ricky was their golden boy. He was talking to his friend Sam when he looked up and saw a guy he didn't know approach TJ. It looked as though they were having an argument of some kind. Some money changed hands, and then "I Who Have Nothing" by Tom Jones began to play as there were audible groans and people began to drift off the dance floor.

Ricky took his drink and moved toward the dance floor to see what was going on. The guy he didn't know was standing with outstretched hands toward a girl whose hands covered her face as she laughed in embarrassment. As she uncovered her face and looked up, Ricky suddenly knew, with an impact that almost took his breath away, exactly what it meant to be struck with an arrow from the bow of Eros. He'd never felt anything like it in his life, and didn't even know it was possible. He'd had girlfriends, and he really cared about a few of them, but nothing had ever affected him like this. Nothing. Ever.

He'd never believed in love at first sight. It seemed an old-fashioned notion. In first lust, maybe, but love? You fell in love as you got to know someone. Yet here he was in its throes. Yes, she was one of the most beautiful women he thought he'd ever seen. He'd seen many. But this… this was that mysterious something that you cannot know exists until you feel it yourself. This was the woman he could imagine in his dream home. He was transfixed.

He watched with the rest of the crowd as the exquisitely graceful creature in the emerald-green dress moved with her partner with such precision, such perfection, you knew they had danced together many times before. The moves obviously had been carefully choreographed. But Ricky didn't really see her partner. It was as though his mind had blocked him out; and all he could see was her lithe, willowy body moving with such suppleness and elegance, it was almost otherworldly. It seemed to Ricky that all else was dark, and there was a spotlight only on her.

His friend Sam elbowed him in the rib and said, "Exhale, dude." Ricky shook his head to clear his mind and vision and watched. Her partner lifted her over his head while she did an arabesque in the air. Her partner then turned around and around again as he held her over his head and covered every corner of the dance floor. Ricky and his friends had to practically duck when she came flying past them, her high heels almost clocking them in the face. Her partner then lowered her to the ground as the crowd went wild with applause.

The couple did a series of disco tango steps to the rhythm of the music, their feet moving so fast, the few other dancers left on the floor thought perhaps they would get tangled up and fall down. Her partner then pushed her out and backs again, over and over. Each time they met in the middle, they were cheek-to-cheek, and they made a large circle again in the middle of the dance floor. They then did a few steps of the hustle to the beat; and her partner turned her in a rapid succession of pirouettes, then threw her toward the dance floor, where she landed beautifully on her rump as she slid across the floor. She landed in a half-jazz split, arms down. And when she landed, she was looking up at Ricky, almost as if it were preordained.

Everything stopped as they looked at each other for a moment. All music, sounds, thoughts, breaths, everything was frozen for a moment in time for the two of them. Her partner then made one last pirouette himself, stomping into a disco pose at the end of the dance to the time of the music, standing over her. There was a half-second of silence at the end, then the crowd went wild. Her partner helped her up from the dance floor.

TJ brought a microphone to them. "That was incredible! May I get your names?" Breathlessly, her partner answered, "Kevin and Isabella!" The dancers smiled.

"Let's hear it for Kevin and Isabella!" TJ didn't have to encourage the crowd. Everyone there was wowed. There were loud cheers and whistles. But Ricky just repeated her name in an inaudible whisper, "Isabella." What a beautiful name. He turned to Sam and said, "Tell me she's not married." Before an astonished Sam could answer, Ricky was striding through the crowd to the door.

He went home and had a drink, but couldn't sleep. The next day, he could hardly eat. Objectively, standing outside himself and observing his own actions, he practically said out loud, "God, man, you're acting like a fool. Get it together!" But 'together' wasn't in the cards. He thought, "If this is what love at first sight does to you, it's pretty freaking scary.

Jesus Christ!" All the clichéd adjectives drifted across his mind – thunderbolt, struck by lightning, bombshell, shock, electricity, and even the romance-novel banality: soulmate. He felt out of control and out of his body. He went through the motions at work and dropped by the Crazy Fox that night seeking her out, but it was practically empty, and there was no Isabella.

Ricky was having another rough night. He could not get Isabella out of his mind. He knew he was in trouble, deep trouble. He drove through the streets near his home, thinking about her, turning that first glimpse of her over and over in his mind. "Get a grip!" he thought. But, no, it was useless. He grabbed a Raspberry Iced Tea at the local 7-Eleven; and when he got home, he shut the door, sat down on the couch, and turned on *Saturday Night Live*, trying to distract himself in order to get some sleep.

Nothing helped, and he spent another night tossing and turning, trying to figure out how to make Isabella his. Sunday was no better. After refusing his mother's invitation to go to church, he did chores and laundry and still could not get Isabella out of his brain. He dropped by the Crazy Fox yet again, but there was no Isabella in sight. He went back home and laid out everything for his workday on Monday.

In the morning, standing under the shower, he thought, "I wonder if I'm in love. Or is this obsession?"

He arrived at his office, got some coffee and, muttering to himself over his fresh cup of coffee, he sat down. He was afraid his coworkers were kind of staring at him a little bit because he was so crazy in love. He turned his office chair around with its back to his coworkers in the glass fishbowl of his office. He said to himself,

"Indeed, I must be."

Just then, his friend Sam walked by. Sam poked his head into Ricky's office.

"What's that?" Sam asked?

Ricky was shaken out of his reverie and turned around.

"What, man?" said Ricky.

Sam said smiling, "I'm not so worried about you talking to yourself, dude. But if you start answering yourself, you gotta get outta here, take a walk, or something."

"Shut up, Sam," said Ricky.

He turned his chair back around to face the Pacific Ocean.

"Hey, don't forget, I set you up with Emily for tonight. Remember? The Fern Bar," said Sam.

"Yeah, yeah, the Fern Bar," said Ricky, not remembering and not really wanting to go, not now.

"Okay, Rick, but don't stand her up. She's Sally's cousin, okay?" said Sam.

"She's a good girl. This is a wife-type girl. Don't fuck it up,

because Sally will skin me alive if you hurt her. I'm not kidding," he cautioned.

"Got it," said Ricky, standing up and ushering Sam out of his office.

"I've got a lot of work to do."

"Are you fishing with your eyes? Because all I see you do is sigh and look out the window at the ocean," said Sam.

"Yes, yes, I'm fishing," said Ricky, shutting his door.

Sam spoke loudly through the door.

"TONIGHT, the FERN BAR, don't fuck it up!"

"Okay, GOT IT!" said Ricky, losing his patience.

His coffee, now cold, held no appeal to him. So he pushed it aside and opened his calendar to review his appointments for the day. On this calendar, he put "Fern Bar" and "Emily" at the seven o'clock slot; and then he promptly put the letters, "I" at the 8:30 slot because he was going to find Isabella.

Then, he said,

"What the hell!"

He smiled to himself and the "I" on the next day, and the next, and next for the next month and so forth. He didn't care. He must go back to where he found her in the first place: the Crazy Fox. He was willing to wait there all night if he had to, every night, until he found her.

By dusk, Ricky had worked a full day. His heart was in his work and he did a good job, and yet, he still was bound and determined to see this Isabella person again, get to see her, get to introduce himself to her. Kevin, be damned. He decided to call it a day.

He shut down his computer and packed up his briefcase. He took a swig of Listerine from the tiny bottle in his desk drawer, ran his hands through his thick black hair, and straightened his tie. He was just going to go meet Emily straight from work. He didn't care about Emily; he didn't care what she thought about him, if she liked him or not, nothing, because all he wanted was Isabella.

Ricky grabbed the keys for the Corvette and headed out to the car. It was a bit brisk that evening, so he slipped on his suit jacket. When he got in the car, he spritzed a bit with a small bottle of Aramis he kept in the glove box.

He wheeled the Camaro onto the PCH and turned at Sunset Boulevard, heading up to the Fern Bar in Hollywood, where he would meet the illustrious Emily, the marrying kind. Or not.

Just as Ricky drove by the Crazy Fox, he pulled into the driveway, on impulse. He parked, and walked in the club. It was before the usual rush, so there was no bouncer yet. He nodded at a few of the acquaintances he had seen there before who were gathered around the pool table.

"All right," he said, trying to walk as casually as possible around the club, looking for Isabella.

A few intimate couples were smooching over margaritas in a corner booth, and stopped like deer at a watering hole to look at him as he walked past. No Isabella. He walked to the back and hung out by the ladies' room for a minute. No Isabella. He made his way to the bar and sat there for a few minutes. Still no Isabella. He couldn't ask for her. "She was Kevin's girlfriend," he thought. He waited a few more minutes and then looked at his watch. He decided he might as well go see Emily.

By the time he drove from the beach to the Fern Bar, he already resented Emily. He knew it wasn't fair. He told himself to be nice to her. It wasn't her fault that he'd fallen in love with someone else and didn't want to be there. Besides, maybe she'd been coerced into meeting him, and was feeling annoyed and resentful as well. They could both make the best of it, have one drink, and be on their way, having made Sally and Sam happy.

He walked into the Fern Bar, a place he really disliked – why had he agreed to come all the way here? He knew instantly that the woman sitting at the end of the bar was Emily. She was pretty, the sort of washed-out blonde type, and she seemed to be in an intense conversation with the bartender, a pony-tailed hippie, as the guy leaned over to light her cigarette. Very reluctantly, he walked over and introduced himself.

"Emily? Hi, I'm Ricky Blake."

She smiled to him, "Oh, hello. So nice to meet you."

He immediately hated the sound of her voice, which he knew was entirely unfair. He just disliked her because she wasn't Isabella. He knew he had it bad. Isabella was like a beautiful virus that had infected every cell in his body, for which there was no cure. He thought, "OK, I just have to be reasonably pleasant for half an hour, and then I can leave."

"Nice to meet you, too."

She turned to the bartender and introduced him as someone she had gone to high school with, had lost touch with, and had just found again. It seemed to Ricky that she had more than a passing interest in the guy, which made him feel greatly relieved, thinking, "I may not even have to stay half an hour."

As they made small talk, her eyes kept wandering to her long-lost friend.

She looked at Ricky and said, "I bet you were pressured into this. It's OK. You don't have to feel any obligation. I was, too. I think we're both here under duress."

Well, she wasn't Isabella, but she was a decent human being. Fate, coincidence, serendipity, whatever you care to call it is a funny thing. Just as he smiled gratefully at Emily, more relaxed now, he looked up and found himself staring straight into Isabella's eyes – eyes as blue and clear and deep as a volcanic lake he'd once seen on a family vacation in Oregon. She was looking at him with both curiosity and amusement. He was embarrassed, and thought he had to let her know he wasn't involved with Emily, and was heartened to see she was alone. But just as he formed that thought, Kevin arrived.

Ricky had always had some pretty smooth moves, but now, in this situation, he felt awkward and uncomfortable. He was damned if he was going to leave without getting Isabella's number or giving her his. And here he was with a blind date that he had no interest in, and who clearly would have preferred to be with the bartender.

"Think fast, Ricky, think fast" were the words that passed through his mind. He watched as Kevin and Isabella slid into a booth with another couple. Emily intruded on his thoughts to excuse herself to go to the ladies' room. While she was gone, he tried to keep his eyes on Isabella without seeming to do so. He took a cocktail napkin from the bar and a pen from his jacket pocket; and hastily wrote down his name, number, and "Friends? Coffee? More?" and folded it.

Just as Emily was returning, she was approached by a friend, who seemed from her body language and loud voice to be very inebriated. Emily introduced the friend and her date, rather reluctantly. This Cassandra and her date were the loud, embarrassing type that made Ricky cringe.

But when Cassandra turned and waved and said, "Hi, Ishabella!" slurring her name, Ricky suddenly liked her just a little bit more. He saw there might just be a possibility here.

Isabella didn't think she knew this very drunk young woman, but she politely raised her glass. So many people knew them as competing dance partners that they felt they knew her. She found it simpler to just be polite. People can be so difficult when they're drunk. Kevin and Henry did the ridiculous bro handshake.

"How you doing, man?" asked Henry.

"Great, great, you?" answered Kevin, nonchalantly getting up to go to the loo.

"Gotta drain the lizard," he said, shaking out his slacks.

Ricky got his chance, and was now looking straight at Isabella. As she felt that someone was watching her, she looked at Ricky and smiled. Then she fixed her eyes on the mirror at the backsplash of the bar just as Ricky looked up into the mirror. Their eyes locked again. A slow, creeping grin involuntarily slid up the side of his mouth as Isabella wrapped her gorgeous lips around her straw, delicately drinking her cocktail. Her eyes were ablaze. "Like sapphires," he thought. "No, that's too trite… like lapis." Then she smiled again, and you could tell that she was having fun with their mirror game. Ricky felt that he was at the center of the universe with her, just the two of them.

Cassandra said loudly, in a bad-drunk whisper behind one of her hands into Henry's ear after Kevin was out of earshot,

"Are Kevin and Isabella dating? Shhhhh!"

"Naw, he's been after that tail for years, but she's not having it," said Henry. "I know he's been after her forever – just can't seem to get it through his head that she's not interested in him as anything but a very good dance partner." That was definitely music to Ricky's ears.

Kevin returned and walked up to Isabella. He held out his hand to ask her to dance. He jokingly dragged an unwilling Isabella to the dance floor. The dance floor was practically empty, and soft rock was playing over the sound system, so they did a loose and lazy disco version of a slow dance.

While they were dancing, Isabella again noticed Ricky, the man who had been staring at her back at the bar in the mirror game. He was smiling at her as she danced. She looked up at him through her dark lashes, and when Kevin had his back to Ricky, she smiled at Ricky over Kevin's shoulder.

Ricky got his green light. He took his cocktail to the edge of the bar, with his back to his date, the bartender, the other couple, everything.

At the end of the dance, Isabella whirled with a flourish, and she accidentally on purpose rolled right into Ricky's arms.

Kevin said, "Hey, man, look out!" to Ricky, who was not at all at fault. Kevin acted like a child while Ricky quietly slipped his phone number into Isabella's lowered palm.

Isabella didn't have much of a poker face, but did her best to conceal her surprise. He had slipped something into her hand.

"Boy, does he have a giant set of cojones," thought Isabella, hoping very much that Kevin would not attack her new admirer.

"Sorry, man, my mistake," Ricky smiled as he walked back to his seat at the bar, thinking this was all too perfect.

Perfect and ridiculous, because Isabella had twirled right into him.

Emily and her long-lost friend seemed enthralled with one another, and hardly looked up when Ricky said a very polite good night. He just shook his head, sighed, caught one more glimpse of Isabella, and walked out the door. He turned to look back one more time, and she was following him with her eyes. Kevin was engaged in a heated discussion with Henry and wasn't paying any attention as Ricky made a hand signal for Isabella, mouthing the words, "Call me!" He was outrageously bold. It made her laugh.

"What's so funny?" said Kevin, now paying attention.

"Nothing. Everything. Maybe the whole scene. It's getting old and tiresome."

Ricky pushed through the doors, leaving the crazy evening.

"Mission. Accomplished," he said under his breath as he stuck his car key into the lock of the Corvette.

Now began the agony of waiting for Isabella to call – *if* she'd call.

Chapter 4

Michael

Customer Service

NOTHING WAS THE same after my brother left. Our room felt strange and empty without him. I had thought it would be great to have my own room, but instead the room felt like a balloon that had been emptied of air. Being a typical self-centered adolescent, I was sure that I felt his absence most, and maybe I used it as an excuse to wallow in my self-pity for a while. There was more space to make a complete pigsty of the room I'd always shared with my brother, and my mother's sympathy was easily evoked.

But my father wasn't having it. Once again, he stepped in to intervene to get his remaining son back on track. He wasn't quite as hard on me as he'd been on my brother. I think he felt that had backfired. But nonetheless, he laid down the law. I was to shower – apparently, I had become a little ripe. I was to clean my room. I was to stop leaving dishes in the sink and having my mother wait on me. And the kicker: he'd gotten me a job. He didn't send me out into the world to find one on my own, as he had with Chris. This time, he was not only going to lead the horse to water; he was going to stand there and make sure that he drank.

My father arranged a job for me with a friend of his from the Elks Club, one Jim Peterson of Peterson's Menswear, who obviously liked my father a great deal. We sat in his office while Peterson and my father made small talk for a bit. Then he turned to me and told me I'd start out at the bottom, in the stock room ,and work my way up. It was that easy.

I had a job. And, to my great surprise, I felt damn good about it.

I arrived very early the next day. I certainly wasn't going to be late. I was feeling all kinds of things I'd never felt before, like the desire to make a good impression and do a really good job. When I arrived at the warehouse and rang the bell to be admitted, the only one there to let me in was Peterson himself. I think he was surprised I'd arrived so early. He said, "Welcome, Kiddo," (he always called me that) and told me to come up to his office on the second floor. "Frick and Frack are always late." I wasn't sure who he meant. "I mean your co-workers, Coach and Todd. Here's the best piece of advice you're gonna get. Whatever those two do, do the opposite and you'll be alright."

And I did do alright. I liked having a job, I liked making money of my own, I handled the razzing by my two co-workers. The better I got at my job, the less I felt at sea without my brother. And I knew both my parents were proud of me. As time went by, I became more confident, more sure of myself, and it felt good.

One afternoon, Peterson asked me to take his very buxom, blonde... um... secretary, Lucille, home. I was to take his gorgeous white Cadillac; drop Lucille off; then take his car to Casa de Cadillac to see his friend, Bob, and get the car serviced, cleaned and detailed. Lucille was outrageously flirtatious on the ride to her place. That was just who she was. I don't think she could help herself. She just exuded sexuality, exuded it through every pore in her body. It guess it was in her DNA. I also knew she belonged to Peterson, and she had me breaking out in a cold sweat. How could I not notice her cleavage and her skirt falling open, and not accidentally? I was relieved when I finally dropped her off.

I brought the car to the dealership, saw Bob, and was treated like royalty because I had Peterson's Caddie. I waited in the VIP lounge and helped myself to too much coffee and too many donuts; and was feeling queasy when one of the managers came in and told me the car had a leak in its rear suspension, and the cost of fixing it would be $2,500. Well, it just so happened that I was in charge of hosing down the parking lot at work. Peterson always parked in the spot reserved just for him, and had there been a leak, I would have noticed.

I was not liking this service adviser so much. I asked him to put everything on paper for Peterson. As I was about to drive away, I let him have it. "I'll give this to Mr. Peterson. I'm sure he's gonna want to know why there's an up-charge on a nonexistent leak that would probably have been taken care of by warranty anyway because the car has less than 4,000 miles and it's less than a year old."

Of course, I told Peterson everything. He was impressed. From that moment on, he took me under his wing, put me on the floor, and told me I had management capacity. Later, he saw that I was a natural at customer service and sales, and gave me sound advice on how to be even better. He helped me to be really good at sales, something I will always be grateful for. I hardly noticed the weeks pass by. I was doing really well, feeling sure of myself and maybe just maybe a little cocky.

I was in the zone. I could sell. I was good at it. And I got to know a lot of people in the business world because I sold them their suits. It was a shock when Peterson died of a heart attack, and Mrs. Peterson sold the store and moved away. But it was easy to get a new job. If you can sell, you can always work; and sell, I could.

I got a job at a car dealership… with a little help from Lucille… several kinds of help. It was not lost on me that my father's insistence that I pull myself together after Chris left, and Peterson's mentoring had served me really well. I will always be grateful to them both… and a little bit to Lucille, too.

HOMECOMING

I remember everything I saw and felt the day Chris came home.

I remember a Dodge pulling up to the house, and Chris getting out in his immaculate uniform and standing in salute as the vehicle passed, and then limping up to the house. What I remember most is how grim my brother seemed to have become. Everyone was emotional: my mother, me and my father, who I had never seen cry, ran out of the house and embraced my brother for a long time as his body shook from sobbing. God bless all of our soldiers. I cannot even begin to put into words my pride for him.

After my brother quietly let us make a fuss over him, he patted my father gently on the arm and silently went upstairs to our room and shut the door.

It was a long time before he left our room, and I gave him the space I thought he needed to be alone. When he came out, he didn't eat or speak much. He'd gone from a boy barely out of high school to a brooding soldier of war, a heavy presence in our home.

But seasons change, as do men. When spring finally arrived, Chris seemed better. He enrolled in some classes at our local community college. He did pretty well. He saw some old friends, was a little less silent, even joked with me. And then, goddamn, my brother won the fucking lottery. He actually won a few million, and he was all over the local news. Reporters interviewed him, and strangers on the street congratulated him.

We went out for a couple of beers one night at a local bar. We were just hanging out, shooting the breeze with a few friends. My brother may have been quieter since his return, but he was still a very good-looking guy, and I think the very fact that he was quieter and still had a lingering darkness gave him a kind of mystique. He was not a boy anymore. When that beautiful girl accidentally-on-purpose flipped that raven-black mane of hers and it splashed in my brother's drink, it set things in motion that in retrospect seem almost inexorable.

"Hey, I know you. You're Chris. I saw you on the news." And with that, the darkness seemed to lift, and maybe he was genuinely happy for some time.

The day he finally brought her home to meet the family, we were elated and very anxious to meet the woman who had made him so seemingly happy, who seemed to be the agent to give us our old Chris back. My mother had prepared for three days straight, and my father had planted two new shrubs in front of our house at the end of the path to the front door.

My mother pressed so much food on Cynthia, we all laughed. My father warned her that the family was crazy – crazy for love, and waltzed her around our dining room table. Chris cut in and dipped her so low, we all thought he'd drop her. But he caught her up in his strong arms and kissed her, and we all applauded.

Some men are born with extraordinary luck. But luck is a funny thing. It can cut both ways. On impulse, my brother had bought a lottery ticket and won. What are the odds?

Now he was in love, and he seemed like a mature version of his old self. And he married Cynthia in a beautiful ceremony and made all of us incredibly happy.

Chris had kidnapped me, insisted that I get in his new BMW, then blindfolded me. I wasn't sure where we were going, but I for sure knew I was getting queasy with all the twists and turns, and was beginning to feel really impatient when the car stopped. Chris came around the car, helped me stand up, and slowly slid the blindfold down my face. I knew we were somewhere on top of Mulholland Drive, and what I beheld was a huge, spectacular, sparkling-white contemporary house, all clean lines and glass.

I was trying to think what the hell we were doing there when Chris said,

"Let's go in."

I told him I wasn't going to break into the house, and he asked me how I felt about using the keys. So yeah, he had bought this gorgeous home for him and Cynthia; and in a very expansive mood, he had also bought me a new car. And over their protests, he had paid off our parents' mortgage.

I was genuinely very happy for my brother. He seemed to have everything one needed to make a happy, successful life: the money, the beautiful girl, the marriage, and a very beautiful home. I had been so worried about him when he was in Afghanistan. Now, seeing how his life was coming together,

I felt such a sense of relief, and both pride and delight in his good fortune. And I hugged him, and almost couldn't let go.

The following year, Chris and Cynthia welcomed their first child, a son. My over-the-moon parents had their first grandchild.

Chris and his wife gave a party at their wonderful home. There were a lot of people, and he was living large and doing it up right. He seemed ebullient and very proud of his home and family. I asked where Cynthia was, and he told me she was busy in the kitchen.

"Hey, c'mon, brother. Let's get you a plate of food."

We entered the kitchen just as a very handsome, tall man with dark hair was lighting his wife's cigarette. There were guests with plates of food careening between Chris and his wife, but Chris looked only at her, and it definitely seemed that something was not right. I heard him whisper to himself, "What the fuck."

As Cynthia was so much into her conversation in the kitchen, she noticed nothing.

Weeks passed, and I couldn't forget that scene. It was indelibly printed on my brain. If I'd only known what was coming...

All of us were at their home when my brother got news that his comrades in Afghanistan had been badly injured, and some had lost their lives. I remember my mom telling him that no matter what was happening in the world, he had a family with a small baby boy now, and that Cynthia had a surprise for him. His wife announced she was pregnant again.

"Beautiful," my brother said, as cold as stone.

It was an emotionally messy scene. My mother told Cynthia not to let him go back, but Cynthia said she couldn't hold him here and that he would do what he wanted to do, regardless of what she said. Then she turned without another word, went to her bedroom, and closed the door.

I've never seen my mother so angry – before or since. My father was furious as well. And me? I felt betrayed. It may have been foolish but that's what I felt, as though he cared more about being with his Army buddies than his own family and his brother. You could see in his eyes that he was determined to go back, no matter what.

He sent pictures back that had been taken in a recovery center. In one, he was with a friend who had lost a leg. Another showed a friend who'd lost his right arm and eye. Chris looked so serious and so determined. He wrote on the back of one, "I'll be home in time."

And he was. After seven months in Afghanistan, he came home in time for the birth of his baby girl.

I bade my time then, and found the right moment to ask my brother to go out and have a couple of drinks with me. After more than a couple, Chris told me he knew I'd invited him out to talk about his experiences in Afghanistan. He went on and told me. "It's a war zone. Have you ever shot or killed someone?" Did I think I could handle that? I didn't say anything, and he went on.

"You see young boys at a window. All kids are born innocent, but at the same time, those bastards are hiding right there and use the civilians as cover. You know in a split second that whole building will be rubble." He shook his head, then continued.

"Or the rage, the inability to have authority over anger, it's illogical, cannot be put in words... that's the most destructive thing in a soldier's life." He told me all this in a voice devoid of emotion and cold as ice. I thought that maybe talking about things would help, but it seemed to me then that he had not and could not release anything, really.

Chris and Cynthia had another of their beautiful parties to celebrate their daughter's baptism. Cynthia liked parties and spending money and having a house full of people. It was never right from the beginning. Now I know Cynthia had my brother marked as an affluent catch before she walked up to the bar and flipped that raven hair into his drink. For her, it was never love; it was luxury.

We had all come to celebrate, but Chris became infuriated with Cynthia when he saw her with a man he didn't know, laughing and drinking. Cynthia told him the stranger was just an old friend from work who now lives just a few streets away. But I could tell Chris was angry – *really* angry.

A few weeks later, I tried to surprise my brother with a deep-sea fishing day trip. I thought it would be good for us, that he'd be able to relax and have a little fun. I thought a great many things. I could feel my brother slipping away again, this time into his own interior. I was almost desperate not to let that happen.

Cynthia opened the door and told me Chris was out back on the patio. As I approached the back yard, I could hear him. His voice was raised, and he sounded extremely agitated.

"No way I have PTSD, no way, sir! I fought for my country, and that's that." There was quiet for a few seconds, then, "I just want it all to be over." I understood perfectly that there would be no fishing today.

Weeks passed, and I couldn't get what I'd heard out of my mind. Maybe I should have told my parents then, maybe this, maybe that, maybe a million different things. But I was trying to protect my parents from heartache. Even to this day, I just don't know. In protecting them, did I seal Chris's fate?

From what I pieced together, the police came to his door and insisted that he open it. Chris tried to sluff things off as just a minor argument between husband and wife. The police must have told him that to his neighbors, it didn't sound so minor. One of them went to find Cynthia while one stayed with Chris, who kept protesting that it was nothing.

Then they told him it was the call from inside his house that had them the most concerned. The other officer returned, and that was that. He was to leave immediately because his wife didn't feel safe with him in the house.

It must have seemed then to my brother that his whole carefully constructed world had fallen apart. Good fortune no longer smiled on him. His good luck now cut the other way, and the wound went deeper than any of us understood.

Chapter 5

Ricky's World

Isabella

ISABELLA KEPT TAKING the napkin out, looking at it, then putting it away again. She told a friend about this mysterious guy. Who the hell was he, anyway? But, secretly, she admired his nerve. But what kind of guy was this? Did he have a brain in his head, or was he just damn good-looking?

Finally, her friend, losing patience with hearing about it all the time, told her to just get up the nerve to call him and find out once and for all.

"That's it, Isabella! I don't want to hear any more about this guy unless you call him."

So, after some indecision on her part and days of mounting anxiety on Ricky's part at the thought he might never see her again, the usually very decisive Isabella, with butterflies in her stomach, took out the folded napkin and tapped his number into her phone. She had the strangest feeling that she was calling into her future.

Ricky was in his office, feet up on his desk, gazing out at the Pacific, not attending to business. He'd been off his game from the time he'd given her his number. Usually a consummate professional, he had been, in his own estimation, behaving like a dopey kid. When he picked up the phone and heard her voice, he knew instantly who it was and didn't need her to say her name. The voice was low and silky-soft, with just that little touch of hoarseness that made it incredibly sexy. Somehow, in fits and starts and a bit of initial awkwardness, they decided to meet at the Blue Coffee at the beach.

From the moment they meet, the attraction is electric and so profound, they are both scared by it. They each feel as though they are being swept away on a wild, unpredictable current, and the only option is to let it take them wherever it will. Ricky finds out she's smart and funny. They both find that, in addition to whatever this crazy thing is, they have a lot in common – food, music, politics, goals.

After an initial awkwardness, they talk easily with one another. Isabella finds that in addition to being smart and articulate with passionate opinions, Ricky is also a great listener. After listening intently, he will ask her intelligent, thoughtful questions about what she just said, indicating to her that he has actually taken a sincere interest in what she has to say.

Ricky can't take his eyes off her. She's just so beautiful. But he also realizes that in addition to the gorgeous package, Isabella is also a person of substance. She volunteers downtown at homeless shelters. In addition to that, she has a great sense of humor and a low, throaty, full-hearted laugh that he finds incredibly seductive. She's actually making a living as an artist, a damn hard thing to do, with showings in galleries in Los Angeles and Santa Barbara.

She has studied in Paris and New York. He has a sudden realization that this one, this ravishing Isabella, is very special; and he's not going to make any moves on her right away. He doesn't want to scare her off and have her think his only interest is getting into her pants. While it may be true that he'd very much like to get into her pants, he wants so much more, and he's not going to screw this up by being a jerk.

He does, however, ask about Kevin. He has to know there will be no impediments to whatever this is. Isabella tells him that Kevin is just a very dear old high school friend, nothing more. But he was a terrific dance partner – and she loves to dance. She also feels protective of Kevin. He'd had a very difficult time with bipolar disorder and anxiety. In their senior year of high school, he had tried to kill himself; he had been on different combinations of medications for years. It seemed now that maybe they had found the right one, and she hoped he would be all right going forward. Ricky is vastly relieved.

They can hardly bear to part. But Ricky, exercising the discipline he really doesn't want to employ, gives her sweet, gentle kisses on both her hands, and they make plans to go to dinner over the weekend.

Bliss

Both Ricky and Isabella each know, without even being able to articulate it to themselves, that something profound and important has occurred in their lives. They are like two interlocking puzzle pieces that fit together perfectly. While each is doing their best not to rush into anything really serious too quickly, it proves impossible. As the weeks pass, they are inseparable, and they know that's the way they want to be forever – inseparable.

Isabella came out of the bathroom, dressed only in Ricky's t-shirt. It was thin with age and V-necked. Her pert nipples practically popped through the soft cotton. She was so tiny, it fit her more like a mini-dress. One shiny, perfectly articulated shoulder poked out of the neck of the shirt provocatively. She was a beautiful creature, to be sure.

She stepped through to the bedroom in the master suite and walked over to the bedside. The bed was a mess, but she didn't care. She grabbed her pink panties, which were hanging from the lampshade, and hopped forward a few steps as she slipped them over her shapely thighs and adjusted them.

She walked over to the stereo, put on a CD, and cranked up the volume. It blared out her favorite Italian song, "Amore, Amore, Amore!"

She caught a glimpse of herself in the reflection of the '50s modern gold, starburst-shaped mirror above the stereo;

and adjusted a wayward curl. She smiled at herself in the mirror.

"Such a pretty mess," she laughed to herself. She hugged herself and twirled around to the music. What was this feeling, besides love? "It's joy," she thought, "pure, unadulterated joy." Ricky made her so happy.

Isabella leaned over and lit the first taper, her beautiful shape then illuminated by the candlelight as she lit the second tall white candle. She straightened the white tablecloth and arranged the red roses a little bit. She set the table with wine and water glasses. Carefully, she poured the Fetzer Merlot, Ricky's favorite, so as to not spot the tablecloth.

Ricky came through the sliding glass doors that led from the patio to the dining area. Dressed in only boxer shorts and a "Kiss the Cook!" apron, he started lip-syncing to "Amore, Amore, Amore", and did a little bump-and-grind to the music while carrying a platter of grilled filet mignon, asparagus, and potatoes. Isabella could not help but laugh as he came toward her for a kiss. He was so silly, so wonderfully silly and funny.

She ruffled his messy hair.

"We're a mess!" she teased him. "A happy, joyful, wonderful mess!"

"Yes, we are, my Isabella," he said as he set the grill platter on the table and whirled her around with one arm, directing the music with the other, singing loudly, "Amore, Amore!" as they slow-danced in the dining room.

"Honey! Honey! The food is getting cold!" Isabella pleaded, giggling as Ricky dirty-danced with her, pressing the small of her back to him. The food smelled so wonderful; she was hungry!

"You are so hot... just like me!" said Ricky.

"Oh my God, Ricky! You're insatiable," said Isabella.

"Mmmm-hmmm, only for you, my love!" he said, kissing her. She kissed him back. She loved him so much. She pushed back a little and put one finger on his lips.

"After dinner, my love," she said. "I'm hungry."

"So am I," he said deeply, looking her in the eye.

They swirled together, dipping lower and lower, eventually disappearing behind the tablecloth, enveloped in each other's embrace.

"We don't want our food to be too hot," Ricky said in between kisses.

Isabella whispered, "I love you, Ricky." She looked deep into his eyes. They had embarked on something beautiful and serious; in that gaze was the promise of total trust and love.

For a time, they kept everything to themselves. It seemed so perfect that each was afraid to let anyone else in. But within weeks, they knew that they had to spread the news.

Ricky was the first to feel he could contain himself no longer. He had to tell his family and friends about how incredibly happy he was. He wanted everyone to meet this wholly extraordinary woman who had made his heart overflow with love. It sometimes felt it would burst if he loved her any more.

Isabella was just slightly more cautious because she knew Kevin would feel that somehow, she was abandoning him. She had been his confidante and friend since they were both fifteen years old. She had always felt protective toward him. She loved him in the way you would love an injured bird, but she had always tried to make it clear to him that as close as they might be, there was nothing more between them but friendship. But things had reached a point beyond which she could no longer keep Ricky just to herself. She wanted her friends to meet the man she adored, and who adored her in turn. She knew most of her friends would be happy for her, but she was wary of Kevin's reaction.

When she told him, they were sitting alone in her studio. He was quiet for so long, she finally said,

"Kevin, aren't you happy for me?"

But all he wanted to know was,

"Is it that slick piece of work from the Fern Bar?"

"Yes and no. Yes, we met at the Fern Bar; but he's not slick, he's wonderful.

You'll like him if you just give him a chance. And if you do give him a chance, I know he'll like you too, Kevin."

He left without a word, but that wasn't so unusual for him when he was in a mood. She thought, "He'll come around," and her attention turned to the email she wanted to send her parents.

It was a long day at work for both Ricky and Isabella, respectively. But Ricky insisted he wanted to meet her at The Garden of Eden on the beach, close to his office.

When Isabella stepped inside, she had to wait for a moment while her eyes adjusted to the dark. The restaurant, lush with greenery, was aptly named. It was cool inside, a veritable oasis from the heat of the valley she'd left behind. Her parents had called from Europe just as she was leaving. The traffic had been terrible. Though she looked truly dazzling, she didn't feel that way. She felt as thought her magenta sundress was sticking to her skin. She was late, she was slightly out of sorts, and she definitely needed a drink.

When the Maitre D' greeted her, she told him she was meeting someone. She had hardly gotten Ricky's name out before he began leading her through the lovely restaurant to the edge of the outdoor patio. Before her, six men, Ricky's friends, were lined up two by two, making a corridor in the sand. There at the end of the corridor stood Ricky at the edge of the ocean, the waves softly licking at his ankles and his rolled-up jeans. Candles lined the aisle the men had created, and each man held a white rose.

Ricky's friend, George, met her at the top step. He led her down to the sand, letting her lean on his arm as she took off her heels, and handed her a white rose, as did each man in turn.

But she hardly saw them. She could not take her eyes off Ricky, who stood quite still, looking at her with such love in his eyes, her heart began hammering in her chest in response.

When she reached him, he handed her a red rose. As she began to question him, he gently put his finger on her lips and began to speak. He had rehearsed his speech numerous times in the mirror before meeting her that evening. He'd written a speech full of wit and humor, but instead his heart took the lead and what he said was...

"Isabella, I think you know you are my world, my every-thing. I wondered," he said, getting down on one knee in the sand while pulling a Tiffany box from behind his back, "if you would do me the very great honor..."

He grinned as Isabella's shoes and flowers dropped from her hands on the sand, unnoticed... "of becoming my wife." He finished, opening the box and revealing a flawless diamond engagement ring. She looked directly into his eyes as he slipped the ring on her finger.

It seemed like several lifetimes before she answered. There was no sound but the waves. She was overcome with emotion, then slowly began to realize that poor Ricky was still on one knee, there in front of all his friends, waiting for her answer. Though he was beginning to blur because she could hardly see through her tears of joy, she was still looking into his eyes.

"Mmmmm hmmm," she managed, nodding her head. "Mmmm hmmm, yes."

Ricky jumped to his feet, wrapping his arms around her as she threw her arms around his neck. He swung her around through the air and kissed her at the same time.

George lifted his glass. "Here's to the quickest engagement in the history of man!" They all laughed and toasted, and none who were there that day would ever forget.

In the next days came the sheer delight of planning their life together and arranging a wedding. Ricky was a bit more conventional than Isabella. She, being an artist, wanted something a bit more unique and colorful, but they easily made compromises and were considerate and gentle with one another. That was, when they weren't eating one another alive with passion.

But there was something Isabella thought might be more problematic. She approached him with a glass of wine when he arrived at her apartment. She handed him the glass almost before he was through the door. He knew her well enough by now to know that something must be on her mind, and that would be something she took seriously.

He looked at her quizzically.

"Sooooo? Something on your mind, love of my life?"

"Yes."

She sat on her couch and patted the seat next to her for him to come sit next to her.

"There's something I want to ask of you, and I will understand if you say no, and I will not be upset."

"Whatever you like, m'lady. Your wish is my command."

"Well, wait until you hear what it is before you say yes. I wondered if you would consider asking Kevin to be one of your groomsmen."

"Isabella, the guy can't stand me. He's so wildly jealous, it's a wonder he hasn't shot me by now. Not that I blame him. You are a prize. I'd be jealous if I were in his shoes, too. He could hardly look at me when we all went out the other night. Then he just disappeared without a word to anyone."

"I know… I know. But I think if he were a part of everything, he would feel so much better, and he wouldn't feel as though he's losing his best friend."

Ricky didn't want Kevin as a groomsman, but she was looking at him with those gorgeous blue eyes; it seemed such a small request in the scheme of things, he just couldn't say no to her. When he acquiesced, she threw her arms around his neck and kissed him.

"Thank you, Ricky. It means a lot to me."

He was surprised by how nervous he felt about meeting Isabella's parents, who were flying in that afternoon from Romania. His parents had loved Isabella the moment they met her. His mother had gone to her gallery the very next day and bought one of her beautiful paintings. He hoped Isabella's parents would feel the same about him.

While Isabella had been putting the finishing touches on her hair and makeup, Ricky was rushing her. The last thing Ricky wanted was to be introduced to her parents after being late to pick them up at the airport. Now they were racing down the 405 toward LAX in his black Navigator, weaving in and out of traffic; Isabella was just a bit scared.

"Slow down, honey! I'd like to live long enough to see my parents and get married."

"I got this, Isabella. You know I'm a professional driver."

As it turned out, he needn't have worried. Her parents were charming people, warm and open and friendly. They embraced him as they would a son. He should have known this divine creature could only have come from wonderful people.

The following days were a blur of happy lunches and dinners, cake tasting and final fittings, preparations, rehearsals, festivities... and laughter and love. It seemed to Ricky that somehow, he had become the most fortunate of men. It was more than he could have ever hoped for. He had great friends. The two families were getting along beautifully despite a slight language barrier, and he loved Isabella with something close to fierceness.

He actually looked in the mirror at himself and said out loud to his reflection,

"You lucky SOB. I don't know what you did to deserve all this,"

and winked at himself before turning away.

The morning of the wedding found Isabella, her mother and soon-to-be mother-in-law at the hairdresser's while Ricky, his father and Isabella's father met at an old-fashioned barbershop, where Ricky's father had been going since he was a kid. Sid, the owner, gave them all a clean shave with a straight razor, trimmed their hair, and provided each with a hot-towel treatment.

Ricky was luxuriating under his when his phone rang. He lifted the edge of the towel to answer. It was Kevin, who explained that his car had broken down and he was on his way to the mechanic.

"What about the wine?" Kevin asked.

"Don't worry about it, Kevin. Someone else can pick it up."

"No... no!" Kevin said emphatically. "I got it, just..."

"What is it, man? What can I do for you?" Ricky was feeling kindly disposed toward everyone this morning.

"Do you think I could borrow your Navigator for an hour? To pick up the wine."

"Sure. No problem. My dad will follow me to your mechanic and we'll drop it off."

"Thanks, Rick. I really appreciate it. I'm sorry for the inconvenience. You guys have so much going on right now, I just... I just want to be of help."

"And you are, Kevin," Ricky said magnanimously. "You've been great."

They were to be married in the Greek Orthodox Church. Isabella had wanted to have their Romanian priest officiate the wedding. From the beginning of the ceremony, the priest explained how the Orthodox wedding will start, that the exchanging of rings symbolized the exchanging of the vows made between husband and wife because marriage is a Holy Sacrament before God, not just a legally binding contract.

After more then an hour, at the end of the beautiful ceremony the priest said:

"May you live as long as you wish, and love as long as you live. You may now congratulate the newlyweds."

Everything up to that point had been a beautiful dream, but when Ricky heard those words, it confirmed his thought that this exquisite creature was truly his wife. He knew in his heart he would love and protect her forever.

When they emerged from the church to greet all their friends and family, who were now assembled in the garden, a cheer went up. George appeared at Ricky's side with a white wicker basket. Ricky reached in and took out a white pigeon, kissed it on its head, and handed it to Isabella, then took the second one out for himself. On the count of three, they released the pigeons and watched as they circled overhead, then flew away.

The wedding party followed the limousine to the Ibiza restaurant for the reception. Mr. Blake drove his wife and Mr. and Mrs. Ionescu in his vehicle. The rest of the guests were already waiting for them at the restaurant, including their longtime family lawyer and dear friend, Jason, and his family.

When they got to the Ibiza, Arman, the proprietor, was waiting for them.

"Right on time!" he said to his staff.

They scurried around, making final preparations for the wedding party. Ricky escorted Isabella out of the car.

"Right this way, my love," he said, helping her get out with her dress in tow.

"Ricky, I need to remove my train," whispered Isabella as she got out of the limo. "Please find mom to help me with this when we get inside," she said.

The ladies retired to the dressing area. When the ladies were ready, Sonia grabbed her husband, and they retrieved the bridal party from the dressing rooms. Two by two, much as they entered the church, the wedding party entered the restaurant and took their assigned seats, as escorted by Sonia and Arman.

Last entered Isabella and Ricky, arms entwined. Everyone stood and clapped for the bridal couple, and Ricky dipped Isabella, giving her a big, romantic kiss.

"Music, please!" Arman said to the DJ.

Mrs. Blake took Ricky by the arm, and led him to the center of the dance floor as Mr. Ionescu took Isabella and led her across to the opposite side of the dance floor.

The parents waltzed with their children for a moment. Then in unison, they led them to their spouses. Suddenly, the room blacked out, and the couple was washed in a giant white spotlight overhead.

The wedding party came to their feet in a giant roar of applause as Ricky led Isabella in their first wedding dance.

"Beautiful," Arman whispered under his breath, wiping a tear from his eye.

After the dance, Ricky thanked everyone for coming and said.

"Let the party begin, this one is for all of you! Oriental Express! Enjoy!"

Everyone applauded and cheered.

Drums began beating powerfully, and four beautiful belly dancers made the way to the center of the dance floor, moving their hips rhythmically to the music. The coins on their waists jingled to the beat, and the wedding guests were amazed at the way they were able to isolate their abdominal muscles in different positions in order to create body curves to express themselves as the music played. Their body language was more than something just sensual; it was emotionally artistic, like a language.

After the belly-dancing show, there was a moment of silence, and then everyone applauded and cheered. The audience immediately leapt to their feet in a standing ovation.

The girls curtsied, and then, again to the rhythm of the music, gracefully made their way off the stage.

Hours of pure enjoyment ended when TJ put on the music from "The Stripper" and Kevin announced, "Okay, guys, now comes the moment you've all been waiting for." He grabbed a chair from a table and put it in the middle of the dance floor.

"This, lady, is for you!" he said.

"Fellas, gather round. Ricky, this is the moment!"

Isabella sat on the chair. Ricky knelt at her feet and slowly, slowly raised her skirt. As he got over the knee area, she couldn't help herself, and covered her face with both hands, laughing.

"Ricky, my mother is here," she laughed through her hands.

Mrs. Ionescu called out,

"Yes, and I'm watching every move!" she laughed.

Ricky slowly worked Isabella's blue garter off of her leg, slowly and to the rhythm of the music. When he was done, he did a comic little strip dance around her, whirling the garter in the air. As the music came to a crescendo, he twirled the garter over his head in three big circles as he turned his back to all his groomsmen and all the single guys at the wedding, and shot the garter behind him to the men. Kevin ground-tackled George for the garter.

"Damn, man," said George, picking himself off the ground, "Are you nuts or what?"

"I told you I wasn't playing," said Kevin, under his breath to George. Then Kevin's face did a hundred and eighty-degree change as he was swinging the garter in the air.

From then on, everything was colors and music and smiles and congratulations. Perhaps everyone felt the wedding and reception was the most beautiful. But Ricky knew that none could compare to his; and no one, absolutely no one, could compare to his wife, his beautiful, radiant, smart, talented, warm, generous, wonderful wife.

At the bridal table, there was a gold, ornate box for people to drop cards, with some including cash, gift cards, and checks. Some older couples came, and they spoke a different language.

"Ti haraua ficiori, s-anchirdaseasca." Smiling, they showed a coin to Isabella and said, *"Aestu iasti di la Baba Sulta ditu Girtii, nu putu tas-ini mirata, Americhia iasti multu alargu ti noi, ama* limbã di mana, *'"Armanamea"' nu cheari!"* and dropped some coins in the box.

Isabella smiled and responded, *"S-bineatz si anchiliciuni di la noi ali Babi Sulti."*

The next couple dropped an envelope and said, *"Felicitari frumosilor, sinteti o pereche minunata."* Isabella said, *"Multumim frumos, ne bucuram tare mult ca ati venit!"*

"What did they say?" Ricky shook their hands, smiled and asked Isabella.

"I'll explain to you later," she smiled. He smiled back.

The rest was an ecstatic blur.

When the evening finally ended and they were about to escape into a waiting limo, they were both a little tipsy. Ricky and Isabella settled into the limo, but Ricky had a surprise for his new wife. The limo took them through winding hills and hairpin turns up to Mulholland Drive. "Isabella, close your eyes and don't open them until I tell you. Promise?"

"I promise."

The limo pulled through a set ornate iron gates onto a circular driveway and finally came to a stop. "Wonder View Drive, sir."

"OK. Now open 'em and see your Wonder View."

When she opened her eyes, it was wondrous. This beautiful house that Ricky has rented commanded a dazzling view; and on this crystal-clear night, with a million lights twinkling in the city far below, they spent their first night as husband and wife, exhausting themselves with pleasure and passion, the first night of the rest of their lives.

"Hey, honey! Look!"

said Ricky, opening the box and pulling out some money and checks. "We're rich!"

Isabella giggled as Ricky spread multiple hundred dollar bills across her lap like a tarot deck.

"Wow!" she said.

"And look, checks!" said Ricky, laughing out loud.

"One from Uncle Herbert for two hundred dollars! One from Aunt Harriet, one hundred dollars! From your Uncle Sol, a thousand! Wow!"

They looked at each other and smiled. Ricky shook the box and heard the coins rattling around. He pulled a handful out, then

held up the coins to the light.

"It's what I thought," he said.

"Gold. I remember them saying something in a different language."

"It's real gold."

"I love those people! Who are they?"

"Romanian-Macedonians," said Isabella, laughing and shaking her head.

"Huh?" said Ricky. "I don't understand."

"Oh, you will," said Isabella, "you will. It's an old tradition from my mom's side."

Ricky said with a smile, "I love your Romanian-Macedonian people."

He then grabbed the bag that had been given by Bertha.

"What's this?" he laughed, "a cake plate?"

"I don't know, pull it out," she said.

Ricky pulled the gift out the bag. In the bag was an ornate gold embossed box.

"What is it?" said Isabella, pulling off the lid.

Inside the box was a beautiful wrapped gold wire case, which held two skull-shaped shot glasses. In the center of the gold case was a crystal skull bottle containing Gran Centenario Tequila. The crystal skulls were accented with gold.

"Wow!" said Ricky.

"Your cousin is wild at heart!" he grinned.

"Look, aw!" said Isabella,

"it even a little skull salt shaker!"

"Yeah, but no limes."

"Wait, wait, nooooo..."

said Isabella, pulling a baggy of cut limes out of the gift bag and laughing.

"This is nuts!" she said.

"That little church going cousin.

Who knew?"

"Hey, what does the card say?" asked Ricky.

"'For your wedding night!'" she said, reading the card.

"Oh, my god, that crazy girl!"

She and Ricky burst out laughing.

"Well, we must oblige," she said.

"Indeed,"

he said, popping the cork. He poured two shots, trying hard not to spill tequila on Isabella's wedding dress.

"Careful!" she said.

He put salt on the back of her hand, she licked it and took the shot and sucked a slice of lime, now your turn she said handed him the shot.they grabbed the limes, sucked them, licked the salt off their hands, and did shots.

"Whoa..." said Ricky.

"That's good stuff." Isabella shuddered.

The next day, at around 10 AM, they drove to their home. Their families joined them for breakfast, bringing with them a huge variety of fabulous breads and pastries. Isabella's parents treated Ricky as if he were the son they never had; and Ricky's parents took such obvious pleasure in their new daughter-in-law, it seemed they loved her almost as much as he did.

The families were enjoying the morning and each other's company when Kevin arrived, his car filled with wedding presents. He announced, laughing, that there were many more he couldn't fit in his car, and that there were still almost twice as many left at the restaurant.

Ricky thanked Kevin for his generous help, and reminded everyone that he had a 4:00 PM meeting to show a property in Malibu. The plan was to take both families to Vegas for the weekend. They would spend the night here on their return, and then he and Isabella would go off to Hawaii for a real honeymoon.

Kevin was licking his fingers. "Hey guys, there's still a load of presents to pick up. They're not all going to fit in my car in one trip. I was kinda thinking about asking to borrow the Navigator one more time this afternoon to just wrap things up at the restaurant. It won't even take me an hour, and you'd be on time for your appointment."

Ricky wasn't crazy about the idea, but the guy really had tried to be as helpful as possible, and he knew Kevin had to be hurting. He had taken Isabella from him. Not that he'd ever had her as more than a friend, but he knew Kevin had always wanted more. So, against his better judgment, he nodded and said, "OK man. But really, one hour, no more than that."

Kevin left, and Ricky thought of a better plan. "Isabella, let's show your parents where we're going to build our house. Dad," he added, "if I can change the appointment to next week, can you show my clients the house I was going to show them today?"

And it was decided. The plans changed, and it made everyone happy. They would all be together when they went to look at the land where he and Isabella would build their home. A home he envisioned where they would make memories together; a place where they would bring up their children and celebrate holidays and anniversaries, graduations and birthdays; where they would have dinners with friends and barbecues with family... All those moments that go into making a life.

He would share everything with her. Their house would be filled with art – her art. And he would build her a studio – a beautiful studio filled with light. Through the years, they would create a beautiful life together. This was only the beginning.

When Kevin got to the restaurant, several of the staff helped him load the gifts into the Navigator. After it was loaded, he popped the hood.

Arman came out of the restaurant.

"Oh hey, Kevin. You need any help?"

"No, I'm good. It was running a little hot, and I thought I'd take a look. But it's fine."

Kevin grabbed the last boxes and loaded them into Ricky's Navigator.

"I'm back!" Kevin announced.

"Yeah, but you're late. I knew you'd be late," Ricky mumbled under his breath.

"Be nice. He's doing us a favor," Isabella whispered softly.

Kevin walked up and put his arms around both their shoulders.

"Everything OK?"

"Great man, really great. Thanks again for all your help," said Ricky, and he meant it.

"Sure. Anything for you guys," Kevin said as he walked toward the door.

"Oh, almost forgot," he added, tossing Ricky the keys. "Have a nice trip." He smiled and walked out the door.

After Kevin departed, the two families piled into his Lincoln Navigator, anxious to have Ricky and Isabella show them the site where they would build their house. Isabella wanted to sit up front with Ricky, almost as though she couldn't bear to leave his side. The mothers sat in the middle; and the fathers were in the back, where they would have a bird's-eye view of the mountain roads and the twists and turns.

After everyone had taken their desired seats, Ricky said, "OK everyone. Here we go!"

As they exited from US 101 to Topanga Canyon and made their way up the mountain, the valley seemed to go on endlessly as they looked to their left.

"This road is like a snake," Isabella's father said, realizing that California was just like back home on mountain roads, except for the tall pine trees.

Isabella turned to her mother. "I can't wait for you to see the land. It's on top of a small hill. It's not big, but big enough for a four-thousand square-foot home. Eventually, we'll put in a pool. The schools are wonderful. It's close enough to the beach, but also the city. And Ricky also said he's going to build me an art studio. You're going to love it."

As she said this, the car went over a very high, rocky incline. Then on the downhill side, they were admiring the beautiful view when the steering wheel locked. Ricky panicked, losing control of the car. He reached down with his foot, frantically trying to push the emergency brake as the car came to a tight S-curve. The weight of the SUV and its passengers and the angle of the steep mountainside was too much for him to brake fast enough.

Time seemed to stand still. A lazy circling hawk was the only witness as the road curved and the Navigator went straight over the edge of the mountain.

Chapter 6

Aftermath

T HE CRASH MADE the local news. It was too tragic and violent a crash, too good a story not to be hyped for days – "if it bleeds, it leads."

"And now, an update on the lone survivor of the 'Malibu Guy' tragedy on Topanga Canyon two weeks ago,"

the news anchor said on the blaring television that was attached to the hospital wall. The television showed horrible images of the black SUV, crumpled like a tin can midway down the mountain, the passenger side totally crushed.

"If you will recall, the realtor Ricky Blake, a.k.a. 'Malibu Guy', lost his entire family, including his new bride of less than 48 hours in a terrible, deadly accident off the Santa Monica Mountains that is still under investigation," said the anchor.

The news report flashed between photos of the accident, ground-rescue crews climbing down the mountain to get to the accident, and wedding photos of the young, beautiful couple.

"Yes, what a terrible tragedy," the blonde co-anchor replied.

"Wasn't the entire wedding party killed? Both sets of parents?" she asked.

The head anchor answered,

"Yes, that is true."

Photos of the wedding flashed across the television screen, showing mom and pop Blake toasting with the Ionescu's at the wedding. Then came shots of Ricky being life-flighted to Cedars Sinai Medical Center.

"How is the 'Malibu Guy' now? Any updates?"

Shots of Ricky being loaded into the ambulance were shown on the screen.

"We have breaking news on the sole survivor's condition," the blonde anchorwoman said.

"And now, to Dr. Parker at Cedars Sinai."

The screen showed a doctor at a podium.

"Mr. Blake has been in a coma and now he is in intensive care. We are cautiously optimistic that he will pull through, but the road to recovery will be long and arduous due to the extent of his injuries and the personal tragedy involved."

Days passed, and his friends took turns looking over him as he lay unconscious in bed.

One day, a nurse was checking Ricky's IV and was in the process of giving him a sponge bath when she heard him say in a hoarse, cracked whisper, "Isabella." She paged his doctor immediately.

When Ricky finally surfaced from the darkness and tried to open his eyes, his lids felt heavy as lead, and it was a huge struggle to wake up, as though he was coming from a million miles away. He could tell it was night by the black sky outside the window to his left. He shifted his eyes to the right and was surprised to find Jason, his friend and their family attorney, dozing in a chair near his bed.

He whispered Jason's name, and Jason came alert immediately.

"Oh, Rick. Thank god."

Ricky searched the room with his eyes.

"Where's Isabella?" he croaked.

Jason didn't know where to start, or how to begin.

"Well, Ricky… first, you need to get better…"

Ricky slowly raised his hand and said with effort, "Jason, I don't need a speech. Where's Isabella?"

That was when, down at the nursing station, they heard his gut-wrenching scream.

Later that month, Jason pulled up at the All Points Rehabilitation Center. When he walked into Ricky's room, Ricky was packed and sitting on the edge of his bed.

"Can we get the fuck out of here now?" Ricky snapped at him.

After getting his pain medication and signing him out, there was nothing left to do but take Ricky back home. When they arrived and opened the door, rather than emptiness, they found his place filled with his friends, who had stocked his refrigerator and cabinets with food and who waited to give him whatever comfort they could – whatever comfort he would allow them to give him.

George walked right to him and put his arms around Ricky's shoulders. "How are you holding up?"

"Like shit."

"I can't even imagine. I am so sorry about what Kevin did."

"Kevin? What do you mean?"

Jason stepped between them. "Hold on, just a minute. Hold on…" but Ricky cut him off.

"What does he mean? What the hell does he mean? Where's Kevin? Where the fuck is Kevin?" his voice rose, alarming his friends.

"Ricky, Kevin is no longer with us." And to Ricky's anguish, the story unfolded.

"Kevin killed himself."

Ricky was uncomprehending.

"Why? Why would he do that? Why?"

"Because of this…"

Jason said, handing Ricky the suicide note.

The note told the story. It wasn't Kevin's intention to hurt Isabella; it was only to kill Ricky. He dropped the note to the floor, strode to the door, and started tossing coats out onto the pavement.

"Get out!!! Get out of my house, all of you. Get the fuck out of my house and leave me the hell alone." And, not knowing what else to do, they did. They left him alone.

The latest tradition in San Fernando Valley of Van Nuys Cruise Night drew several dozen, if not more, vintage cars. So many spectators showed up to enjoy the event. This group of car enthusiasts put a lot of work and money into those cars to let them just sit at home; and some update their cars with racing motors, batteries and hydraulics. After cruising Van Nuys Boulevard, some drivers pulled over in their cars and posed for photos with friends. Some hopped their cars a few feet in the air as they rode along the boulevard.

Gene and Frank had been following this red Ferrari, discreetly, in their black-and-white for a few blocks. They were following, but not following. Gene's fingers flexed on the wheel, tightening and loosening his grip as he waited for the light to turn green so that he could catch up with the car at the next intersection.

"Fancy," said Frank.

"Dig that crazy logo on the back of the car." He pointed out that the Ferrari had a silver Mustang logo on the back of it, too; but the Ford Mustang logo was upside down and calf-roped, all in silver.

"Very funny… but I don't know if it's the right time and place. I wonder if those guys from the 'Mustang Club' noticed it… That's too much!" said Gene.

Frank called in the license plate number of the Ferrari on the radio. "California plate BR5265, copy?" he said.

"Roger that," Sheila said.

"Run 'em 10-28, and get back to you."

"Gracias," said Frank.

"De nada," said Sheila.

As the light turned green, a car club of Mustangs pulled up and around the Ferrari.

"Uh oh," said Gene. "Looks like we're about to party!"

A few Mustangs cars were right on. Frank whistled under his teeth as a cherry red one zoomed past him.

"Cherry, 1968. Nice."

The Ferrari driver had the top down; and the red Mustang was a convertible, too.

The driver of the Mustang was a good-looking blonde cat.

"Hey, man," she said as she revved her engine at the light. "Your logo sucks!"

The gentleman in the Ferrari rolled down his passenger window a little bit just so you could see his forehead and his big black glasses. He said eloquently, in a heavy accent,

"No, no, I'm afraid it is your puny Mustang that sucks." Then he rolled his window back up and waited patiently for the light, grinning.

"Hey, pretty boy!" said a good-looking kid, driving the blue Mustang that was boxing him in on the other side.

"You're looking kind of hot! Let me cool you down a little bit!"

"What?" said the guy, half-rolling his window down again as the car club, which had him fully boxed in now, roared their engines as the light just turn green.

"I can't hear…"

Just then, a Cadillac pimped to the bone said to the blonde lady in the red Mustang,

"I got this baby!" Smiling, he took her spot on the left side of the Ferrari. Then he lifted his car's passenger side up using hydraulics and, just like a dog taking a leak, sprayed motor oil all along the side of the convertible.

The Ferrari guy got a face full of the motor oil until the sprayer ran out of juice. Then the oil gave one last pump just as he was opening his mouth to say something. That was it, and they took off in a howling fit of laughter. The Ferrari driver threw down his glasses in fury.

"You!!!!" he began, but the guys were now too far to hear any of that.

Frank and Gene started laughing so hard in the cop car that Frank's side was beginning to hurt.

"Oh, that was so bad, so good," said Gene, wiping the tears from his eyes.

"What can we arrest him for?"

"Vandalism? 594?" Frank said.

"594, right."

The cops were just about to pop their siren when a car parked on their right started blowing its horn. They looked over and saw a man passed out, head on the steering wheel.

"Code 3, Frank," said Gene.

"You got it," said Frank, pulling over the police car, lights flashing.

"Sheila, Code 3," said Frank.

Gene got out of the car. "May need to make it a 10-54." Frank felt his neck. "Nope, 10-50, he's still with us."

As Frank got out his flashlight and directed it into the guy's car, he saw cocaine paraphernalia all over his lap. Frank gently pushed back his torso, and the horn stopped blowing. The guy's nose was covered with white powder, and his nose was bleeding.

"Gene, call 11-41," said Frank, sure that he has Od'd, or was on the verge of it.

"You're one lucky som'bitch, old buddy."

He looked at all the drug paraphernalia surrounding the car seats. He checked the registration from the glove compartment. Ricky Blake was the name on the driver license from his wallet.

This was to be the first of many times Jason would get Ricky released and kept out of jail. By the sixth time, he was coming to the very sad conclusion that Ricky might be beyond redemption. What had so injured his body seemed to have done so much more than that to his spirit. Maybe it was too much for one person to bear.

The last time Jason saw Ricky, he could barely walk when they released him. As they stepped out into the wee hours of the morning, he took Ricky by the elbow to guide him, and Ricky shoved him away.

"I don't need your help."

"Well, you're going to need it to get home because the car has been impounded."

"Really? How are we gonna get it out?"

"I don't know, Rick. They also suspended your driver license! I got a family to get home to, a family that's getting a little tired of being woken up in the middle of the night. I have a firm to run in about three hours. Let me drop you at home and we'll figure something out."

He had no intention of telling Ricky then that he hoped they'd never give him the car back. There was a good chance he would drive it again, and he'd kill either himself or someone else.

Ricky was filthy and he smelled, but he didn't seem to notice or care. Jason drove by McDonald's and got Ricky something to eat. When he pulled up in front of Ricky's place, he wasn't sure he should leave him, but he had to get his twins to school.

As he pulled away and looked in his rear-view mirror, he saw a man so emaciated, he looked like a scarecrow, his once-beautiful clothes hanging onto his body like old drapes.

Jason kept Ricky out of jail for months. The judge took into consideration his lack of a criminal record and the circumstances of the tragedy, but warned Ricky he'd throw the book at him if he saw him in his courtroom again. And though Jason's wife had run out of patience with the middle-of-the-night phone calls and the stress her husband was sustaining in his concern for Ricky, Jason wasn't ready to give up.

He remembered clearly when Ricky's father, Larry, hired him to be their family lawyer decades ago when Jason was young and just beginning his law practice. Ricky's father had taken a chance on a young lawyer almost fresh out of law school, and his recommendations to business friends had helped Jason build his practice.

Many years later, he had confided to Jason that he had prostate cancer. But he reminded him to say nothing to Ricky or to his wife; and had him promise that he will take care of them, especially Ricky. Larry had told him, "Treat him like he's your own brother." And Jason had made that promise. He knew Larry had just wanted his family to take joy in Ricky's wedding.

When they left the courtroom, Jason told Ricky he was taking him to rehab. After a heated argument, Jason finally lost his patience.

"You go to rehab right now, or so help me, I'll drive you to county jail and you can stay there. This is it. Decide now. It's rehab or jail."

Within three months of visiting Ricky at rehab, Jason was there to pick him up. Ricky was in a foul mood, complaining about how pathetic everyone and everything had been in this "hellhole." Jason ignored him as he drove in silence, reminding himself to be patient. He stopped at a fast-food place and took him to get something to eat.

After they ate, Jason excused himself to go to the men's room. As soon as Jason was gone, Ricky stood up and walked out of the restaurant.

Hell

Ricky was lost to himself, to his friends, to life. He hit the skids hard, hardly knew the difference, and cared even less. He was an alcoholic, drug-addicted walking corpse. Lying face-down on Ventura Boulevard, he was one of those guys people walk past and shake their heads at, thinking there's little hope for this human being who had turned into not much more than a pile of rags. He was so addled and his memory so soaked in alcohol, he hardly knew where he was or where he was supposed to be. He didn't remember if he even lived anywhere. His diet consisted mostly of dumpster diving when he had the energy; and alcohol, which he bought with the spare change people gave him. He drank to wake up and drank to go to sleep, he drank to forget, he drank to kill pain. He drank. It was his main activity – scoring change to buy something to drink, drinking, sleeping it off and waking to do it all over again. It was his new painful life.

Months passed, and Ricky awakened early one morning to find himself face-down on the sidewalk somewhere in the San Fernando Valley. He slowly opened one heavy-lidded eye to see a white pigeon standing just two feet away from his face. The bird was totally still and silent, and seemed to be looking all the way down to his soul, or what little was left of it. While the other birds scurried about looking for seeds, this one took silent measure of him. They stared at one another for a long moment, neither one moving.

Memories of him and Isabella releasing the white pigeons on the day of their wedding play over and over in his mind like a film on an endless loop. Each time he whispered her name, "Isabella", again and again and again...

He stumbled into a seedy Burger King bathroom with visions of Isabella still dancing in his mind. He stared at what seemed a stranger's face in the mirror. His hair was long and filthy. His hands were black with grime, the nails split and broken. His face was a mask of soot, dirt and despair, pain etched into his features. When he recognized not the face, but the pain in his eyes, he started to weep, the tears making tracks down his filthy face, revealing some of the color beneath the dirt.

He gripped the edge of the sink and stared long and hard at what he had become. He turned on the hot water and squirted some soap on his hands. For the first time in a very long time, he tried to clean himself up.

Looking down at his ripped, ragged backpack, he reached down and took out a pair of scissors, and began to cut off some hair. When he was done, he looked shorn, like Joan of Arc, his hair very short and chopped. He filled the sink with hot water and scrubbed his head with the hand soap. When he was finished, he looked at himself in the mirror.

"There you are, Ricky," he said to the man in the mirror. "It's about time."

But a moment of brief recognition isn't enough to sober up a dedicated alcoholic like Ricky. And given a partner with whom to utterly dissipate himself, Ricky rededicated himself to being totally numb.

Jose, another denizen of the streets, walked by the little space Ricky had made for himself, took a look a Ricky, pulled a pint bottle from a paper bag, and handed the bottle to him. Ricky took it without a word, wiped the top of the bottle with his sleeve, and drank long and hard, feeling his insides warm up. His fingernails were black once again, his clothes black and tattered.

"Merry Christmas," said Jose. "You look like something a dog vomited up."

"Who cares?" Ricky responded.

"Not me, not me. But if you don't wanna die out here. You better follow me, let's get free breakfast and hot coffee. We'll save the rest of this hooch for our demitasse."

Ricky had no idea where Jose was leading him to, but he was willing to go. When he stood up, his pants almost slid down around his ankles. His belt was gone, as were his shoes, his wedding ring, his phone, his apartment, friends, everything. Gone as if they'd never existed. Jose handed him a bungee cord from an old shopping bag he was carrying to hold up his pants.

It was the dispossessed following the down and out as they trudged up Van Nuys Boulevard, Ricky in his stocking feet on the cold pavement. They went to the back of a car dealership, and Jose announced they had arrived.

"Where are we?" Ricky asked, totally at a loss.

"I told'ya about this place. The dealership. You stay here and let me go in. If we both go there, the sales people will catch us and throw us out. I have this down. Be right back."

As Ricky watched from the bushes, Jose slipped in through the back door, and miraculously returned with two fancy steaming cappuccinos and two donuts, one stuck in each pocket.

Ricky, having really expected nothing, registered surprise.

"Well damn, I didn't think you could do it."

"And now for a real delight, a concoction of my own." He poured Scotch from the pint they'd shared into the two coffees.

"Scot-puccino, my good man. And after this, we're gonna get you some shoes."

Michael had just comeback from a test drive and parked in the back when out of the corner of his eye, he saw two homeless men scurrying around the corner of the building. He took a deep breath, shook his head, and walked back into the dealership.

On a cold morning a few days later, Jose and Ricky were standing just inside the 405-freeway entrance, begging for change. They somehow fashioned a sign that said "Merry Christmas", and they each held a big cup that now served as an improvised change bucket.

A car pulled up. It was George, with a couple of Ricky's erstwhile friends. George made it a rule not to give to homeless men, thinking the money would be used for drugs or alcohol that would further their harm.

But there was something different about one of these guys. He took another look. The man's eyes seemed so familiar somehow. Suddenly, George became speechless. He wanted to say something, but no words came out of his mouth. He struggled to get out his wallet and ignored the honking drivers behind him. Once he pulled out all the cash he had, George stuffed it into the cup the astonished Ricky was holding in his hand.

As he pulled away, his friends asked him if he'd lost his mind.

"No. That was Ricky, we have to go back right now!"

His friends protested that the man they'd just seen couldn't possibly be their old friend Ricky. But George, in tears, insisted and said they better call Jason right away.

They made the first exit at Victory Boulevard and drove back, parked in a small lot nearby, and called his name.

Ricky and Jose had already taken off with their newfound wealth to purchase some serious stuff. As they ran, Jose yelled, "Fucking miraculous, man!"

Chapter 7

Searching

J ASON AND MOST of Ricky's friends had searched for him tirelessly for months after he'd disappeared. There was no way they were going to simply let him drift away. But as the months went by, even a private detective in the employ of Jason's firm came up with nothing. They didn't give up. Their search took them all over, including downtown LA and all the missions and shelters on Los Angeles Street.

It had never occurred to any of them that he could be right under their nose in the valley. George and Jason came back day after day to the ramp where George had seen him. They asked around to find out where most of the Valley homeless congregated, to no avail. He'd vanished again like a ghost.

Jose and Ricky were almost giddy with the thought of the drugs they could buy with their newfound "wealth", and Jose said he knew just where they could find such a smorgasbord. They waited at the edge of the parking lot until a silver Lincoln pulled into the lot.

"There's our man," said Jose, and walked up to the passenger window. "Hey, Jack."

Whoever Jack was rolled down the window. "Hey, long time no see. What can I do for you?"

Flashing their funds, Jack, who'd thought they wanted something in the ten-dollar range, instantly became more interested when he saw they had something serious to play with.

Jose selected "some of everything", which included uppers, downers, all-arounders, some crack and some weed — everything they would need to "enjoy the Christmas."

Jack's compatriot, Mo, had exited the car and gone into a pawn shop. He came out in a hurry, behaving strangely and with his hand in his pocket. "Let me in, fast! Let's go, let's go, let's go!"

Jack told Jose that they had to go. Jose asked if he could just drop him and Ricky off by where they stay, and the four men quickly pulled away.

The man inside the gold-and-coin exchange had pushed the silent alarm. "Yes, officer. We've been robbed."

Jack pulled around to the back of the car dealership. "This is where you guys make your lair?" he asked.

"Yeah. Thanks," Jose answered.

Jack looked at Mo and asked, "Where is my share?" Mo took some silver and gold coins out of his pocket and gave them to him.

"That's it? All right, this is your stop, too. Out!"

Mo got out reluctantly and stepped back as the car sped off. Then he turned and watched as Ricky and Jose found their little niche in the bushes behind the parking lot and settled in. Turning their backs to the traffic, they began to partake of their new stash.

The alley was pitch-black. It was overcast that night. There were no street lights, no moonlight, no nothing. But Jose was interrupted by the smell of someone's boozy breath and the hands that was assaulting him in his sleep.

Jose was face-down. He'd been in jail before, and was not going to be made a punk. Someone had his hands in his pants pocket. He hoped it was just money he was after, and not his junk, or the stuff. He had to get out of this vulnerable position, so he did what his instincts told him to do. He pushed himself up, push-up style, with the full force of his body, to a semi-standing position, throwing his assailant backward as he stood.

The men tussled then in the darkness, and something heavy fell on the ground. The attacker felt around for it for a bit, but could not find it in the dark, with Jose wailing on him as best he could in the darkness.

All of a sudden, there was the unmistakable sound of the flip of a switchblade. Before the attacker knew what happened, he felt a slash and a sting on his face. When he felt his face, it was warm and wet. His primordial instincts kicked in, and he charged at Jose. Jose was used to defending himself, but his attacker was so manic, so crazed, so aggressive, he began jabbing at him with the knife.

The attacker ran off, and Jose grabbed for his wallet.

"You motherfucker, you got my money!" said Jose, running after the man down Van Nuys Boulevard.

Jose caught up with him at the bus stop, where there was light. He grabbed the man and turned him around to threaten him with the knife.

"Give me my money, motherfucker!" screamed Jose. Nobody robbed Jose. Nobody. When he turned the man around, he said, "Of course, it had to be a lousy motherfucker like you," flashing the knife in the light.

"Bring it on, you pussy," said Mo.

"Give me my money back, motherfucker, and I will let you live," said Jose.

"Make me," said Mo.

The two men fought again, but this time, it was for the knife. Mo was the stronger of the two. Jose made a wild swing at Mo. Just then, Mo grabbed his arm, turned him around quickly, and shoved him into the bus stop, impaling Jose on his own knife.

"You fucking asshole," Jose screamed, falling into a slump at the bus stop.

Mo reached into Jose's front pockets for the drugs. Jose, who had taken the knife in between his rib cage, was struck in the heart. Mo pushed him over and onto the bench. To all the world, he just looked like another drunk person, passed out for the night at a lonely Van Nuys bus stop.

Mo turned and ran; all one could see of him was heels and elbows as he quietly dashed off into a back alley.

Early the next morning, the first cadre of morning maids making their way to their Encino assignments made the grisly discovery of Jose, now surrounded by a pool of black blood on the sidewalk.

Ricky woke up the next morning cold, stiff and the worse for wear. Wretchedly hungover from all the many substances he'd imbibed the night before, he was dehydrated. His lips were parched, dry and cracked.

He looked around for Jose. That was weird; no Jose anywhere. He called out to him, but there was no answer. He desperately needed something to drink. He didn't think he'd ever been this thirsty in his entire life. But there was no Jose to sneak in and get coffee. Where the hell had he gone?

He got up the nerve to slip in the back door, just as he had seen Jose do many times before. There was a salesman standing there, tall with dark hair. The man may have noticed him out of the corner of his eye, but he said nothing, smiled, and turned to look out the garage bay doors.

If Ricky hadn't felt so desperately dehydrated, sick and hung over, he would have retreated right away. But his monumental thirst and the feeling he was going to be ill if he didn't put some liquid into his body would not allow him to retreat. He grabbed two cookies and two bottles of water from the glass-encased fridge, and quickly slipped back out the door.

Chapter 8

Sales Meeting

Cars and Men

I PARKED MY car at the back of my car dealership. I was walking fast so I wouldn't be late for the Friday morning meeting. The tedium of the sales meetings would drive me crazy not because of the job, but because of the way the managers abused their power. I felt stuck. I had a wife and children who I loved and needed to support. I couldn't just walk away from it, but I'd be damned if I could see myself doing this for the rest of my life.

We got the same fucking talk I had heard a thousand times. The managers had their favorites, and they spoon-fed them. The salesmen weren't that great at sales, but they were great at knowing which side their bread was buttered on. They were on their managers' side, and they made sure to make themselves their protégés and talk trash about the rest, just like little boys bullying the one they didn't like. It made it very personal.

Mark, the general manager, turned to me. "You have to be with a customer, or in search of one all the time. Are you with a customer right now? Are there any customers in here? Then what are you doing? I expect you on the floor or on the lot. Do we understand each other?"

"Yessir," I said, just throwing my half-filled, perfectly flavored, much-wanted coffee.

Mark said, "Sales meeting in ten minutes, main conference room. You got me?"

"Sure," I said.

I was always right on time for the meeting. Mark was ex-military; and timeliness was everything to him, next to sales. I got a seat and looked around at the young, clean-cut crew that were my sales associates.

"Good morning, everyone," Mark said, "This weekend is crucial. We're set to beat last month's sales," he said, "which is good. But we can't fail. We have to do better this month. As you know, December is a tough month for car sales, with all the holidays that November, we had Black Friday, and we're going to have to beat that. Sales are looking good this week, but we can't rest on our laurels. I know we can beat last month's number, but I can't do it by myself.

"On top of that, corporate has issued us a new challenge. We not only have to beat last month's totals, but we also need to beat last year's numbers. Remember your four-square. I expect no more shortcuts. Do you guys understand?" he said.

God, it was torturous. Some of us nodded and some were clapping loudly. Of course, they were his puppets.

"Use the four-square as your bible. Understood? So, with that said, remember to smile, make eye contact, find out what the customer wants and needs, listen more and talk less. That's why God gave us two ears and one mouth. Get out there, sell yourself and sell your dealership, and you'll succeed. And remember, at all times, you are either with a customer, or in search of one. Got it? Go get 'em!" he said, clapping his hands.

It was such drivel. It was embarrassing that grown men had to listen to this crap.

The sales staff started clapping, but he interrupted. "And remember, whoever beats their sales goal... the bonus is for everyone, but not everyone will reach it. But for those who do, let's just say they'll have a nice paycheck for Christmas! Got it? Good!"

We had changed some GMs before, but for this guy, the best fucking therapy was to be in control. Some salesmen looked at one another, a little confused perhaps. But we clapped like hell, anyway, if only to seem like team players. It was fucking depressing.

"Great. Now go get 'em, tigers!" Mark said, standing up in order to indicate that the meeting was over.

As I was getting up to leave with the rest of my co-workers, Mark pulled me aside.

"Wait here a minute, Michael," he said.

"Yes, sir?" I replied.

"I have to tell you something. I have a problem."

"A problem?" I asked.

"Yes, Michael, I have a problem. I have a problem with you missing for long periods of time, taking long breaks, sometimes an hour, an hour and a half. I don't know what the hell you're doing and I don't care, but you're taking too long of a break. You need to be here. Because your numbers, my friend, they don't look good. They are low and I have to write you up! I'm only going to talk to you about this one time."

I nodded. If I'd opened my mouth to speak, I would have told him to go fuck himself.

"Let me ask you this. Yesterday, for example, from two to four, you were not here. Where were you? With a customer?" he asked.

"Yes, Mark, I was with a customer." I lied.

Mark was not born yesterday. "Okay then, what happened with the customer?"

"He said he's going to bring his wife later, so she can drive the car, too."

"If that happens again, when a customer leaves without talking to me, you go with them, too. Is that clear?" Mark demanded. "That's all."

I was just boiling inside. I had to get a grip on my emotions. I was so furious, I just felt like punching the guy, punching the wall, whatever. Okay, yes, yesterday I had to pick up my girls from school and drop them off at Grandma's because my wife could not leave work.

I slipped into the restroom and splashed cold water on my face. I put my face a little closer to the mirror when I was drying my face.

"Okay, let's turn the switch on again. God, how I hate it." Waving my hand over my face, I turned my sad face into a happy face, like the ancient Greek theater masks, Comedy and Tragedy. "I still fucking hate it," I said, smiling, but at least I could put on the front of giving a damn. But if this were a comedy, it was a very dark one, for sure.

I headed to the customer's lounge to get a coffee from the machine. When I entered, the newscaster on the overhead TV said,

"A latest update on last night's incident. They found a homeless man slumped over a bus stop, an apparent stabbing, a homicide. They don't know the motive yet. The man had no identification on him, so they are calling him a John Doe…"

I shook my head. There was a lot of misery in this world. I was holding my coffee when I saw the homeless guy I'd seen before peeking into the area. I instinctively grabbed a donut and walked to the door.

"Here, man," I said, handing him the donut and my coffee. "Something that will hopefully warm you up."

The man smiled and said, "Wow, thanks, man," and I saw him going behind the dealership, a place where I guess he kept his stash.

Chapter 9

Merry Christmas

"I WONDER WHERE Jose is?" Ricky said to himself, and then took a sip of his coffee. "Ah, hair of the dog that bit ya." Out of the corner of his eye, he noticed Jose's brown backpack. "Huh, that's weird, he left it here? Huh. Ooh, I wonder if he's got something in here?" Now he was taking to himself.

Remembering that sometimes, his pal stashed goodies in there, he looked around, knowing that if Jose caught him going through his things, he'd kill him. When he lifted up the bag, Jose's portable radio was underneath.

"All right, man, rock and roll, let the party start!" he said to himself. He put on the radio, and "A Song For You" by Celine Dion was playing.

"Ooh, pretty," he smiled to himself as he rummaged through the bag. "No food," he thought sadly. "But hey, what's this?" He held up a fresh pint. "More juice!" He was just glad for the alcohol.

Later that night, after selling 2 cars that day, I clocked out for the evening. I was walking to my car when I heard a man mumbling to himself. "I hate you, Kevin. I never liked you, never. I never, ever, ever liked you. And now, I'm gonna kill you. Except I can't kill you, because you're already dead," and then came both sobs and laughter.

Very worried, I peeked back down the alley. It was just the same homeless guy, talking to himself. I felt terribly sorry for him. Sometimes, having a rough day oneself will make a person have more empathy than usual.

"Hey, man, good evening. How are you?" I said. I looked down and noticed that the man's pants were ripped all the way, almost from the pocket to the knee, and his white thigh was exposed. It was a cold, foggy southern California night, too cold to be exposed to the elements.

"I don't guess… I mean…" I said. "Look, I have some jeans and stuff I was going to give to the church that I've out-grown, but uh… would you like some? Because it gets pretty cold at night, and I think they'll fit you."

"Want some?" the man offered a forty-ounce Miller High Life.

"No, thanks, man, I'm good. I have to drive home to my girls. But thanks…" The guy was cradling the forty-ounce.

"Well, okay, man. I guess I'll bring the pants."

I went to my car and drove into the alley. I pulled up near enough to the guy to be of help, but not to scare him. I pulled the white plastic kitchen trash bag of clothes I was going to donate to the church homeless program. I felt like I could do the charity work just as effectively right there on the street, that Jesus would see all that and approve it.

"Here you go, man," I said laying the bag of clothes next to the man. "Pick and choose what you want. Hope this will help, and Merry Christmas to you."

"Merry Christmas," the guy responded.

"By the way, what's your name?"

The guy paused for a long time. In some ways, he had almost forgotten. It had been such a long time since anyone had called him by his given name.

"Um. Ricky," he said. "It's Ricky."

"OK, Ricky, mine is Michael."

"OK, Michael."

Next morning, I arrived at work, bright and early - 8:15 A.M. sharp. I was determined to have an excellent day. My personal excellence was something I was committed to, whether I hated my managers or not.

I parked my car and walked across the alley to the back door of the dealership. A figure caught my eye. It was Ricky, off in the distance, in his regular place. Only this time, he was standing and I could see he was wearing his new jeans.

"Mornin', Ricky!" I said, smiling to myself as I walked in to the dealership.

Ricky raised his coffee cup, having already helped himself.

Maybe there was hope, after all. As I walked into the customer lounge through the back door of the dealership, the news announcer blared over the TV, "And in the latest news, another homeless person was found murdered on Van Nuys Boulevard." I fixed my coffee, turned, and watched the news for a second. Then I clocked in.

"Wow, man. Wow," I said under my breath. "That's weird."

What Now?

The meeting started with the introduction of a few new sales people, including Freddy, who was not a "Green Pea". He was coming from a different dealership, where he had been the top salesperson. Mark, the general manager, followed up with the differences between the leasing of a new car versus the purchase. "Don't forget to let the customers touch the leather and inhale the new car smell, then show the features and functions, and explain their benefits. After the test drive, bring them inside and start your four-square as I taught you, with more down payments and higher payments. Then you just shut up. Don't say a word; the first one who opens his mouth saying any numbers loses. If they say 'no lease' don't argue with them, but give them my speech.

"Now let me ask you guys this. When you go out with your friends at a bar and see a beautiful lady alone, would you approach her and say 'Hello. I want to marry you!'?"

Everyone, of course, shook their head and said "NOOOO." I hated being spoken to as if I were thirteen years old.

"The same goes for buying a new car! You have to explain to the customers that it is better to lease the car first for 3 years so you can get to know the car better, like a boyfriend or girlfriend. After that, if they really like the car, they can buy out the lease since they already paid for half of the car anyway, and now they are happily married!"

Everyone started to applaud and cheer him on.

"If you can't get a commitment from them to buy a car right now, turn it before you burn it! Let's go out there and make some money! Go get them, ladies and gentlemen!"

After the meeting, Freddy asked me who the three stooges looking at us are, and who are probably talking about us. I told him that they are the manager's favorite salespeople. That's why they are selling 20 to 30 cars a month; it's because of their strong friendship with the manager. It is not about what you know, but rather who you know.

"Watch me. I'm gonna beat them. I'm going to sell 40, 50 cars. You will see!"

I told him how impossible that would be since no one has ever sold that many cars at this dealership, even with the help of the managers. "But hey, if you can be the first, go for it."

Freddy was now sharing with me his secrets on how to deal to a person of any ethnicity. He told me, "You have to connect with them in the first few minutes. If they say they are from Greece, you should tell them that your grandfather was from Greece, and say a few words in their language. If they say that they are from Lebanon but born in Paris, then you should say a few words in French and end up in Arabic."

"I understand," I said, "but I don't speak those languages!"

"Don't worry," he said, "Just turn it over to me and you'll get a half-deal. Half is better than nothing, like Mark was saying in the meeting."

I start smiling, but at the same time, I have to agree with him that no matter what it is, you have to believe in it.

Some sales people were outside when an old pimped Cadillac pulled in. The driver said to them, "Hey, who is your general pimp cause you all look to me like my prostitutes waiting for a customer! You better get me your pimp right now, bitches!"

One of the favorite salesmen who was close by went straight to Mark and told him that the customer was terribly rude to them.

Mark asked him, "Which customer? The one with Freddy!?"

The salesman said, "Yes!"

"Okay, let's see how good Freddy is."

"But Boss, they were very rude. They called us bitches and prostitutes, and they called you a pimp!"

"What?" He started laughing.

"Yes, Boss!"

"That's okay, they will pay for that," he said, and started smiling.

After 15 minutes, Freddy came back from a test drive on a black-on-black MBZ S550. They were smiling and went straight to the showroom floor, where Freddy invited them into one of the private offices and asked how they wanted to register the car.

The short one said,

"I'm the Boss, what do you need?"

"Sure," Freddy said. "Let me help you fill out your application. Is your address the same as the one on your driver's license?"

"Yes."

"And your job position?"

"What do you mean, job position'? Do I look like a person who has a regular job to you?"

"Oh, I see." said Freddy. "But I have to put a title for your position. Let me see, Entrepreneur at Sunset Strip 88 in Los Angeles?"

"Yes, that's right. Now you're talking," said the second guy. "He's my Boss!"

"I know," said Freddy. "I'm here to help you guys because a lot of customers don't know that you can make payments on a newer car and don't have to pay cash for the car. Put some money down and finance the rest of the car in small payments."

"Yes, that's what I want."

"I know your business runs on cash, and you need the cash. Like I said before, I'm here for you. Please, I need your signature here and there. Thank you. Give me a few minutes, and I will submit this to the bank."

"Great," they said.

The short one said, "Call the bitches. We're going to Vegas tonight!"

After less than one hour, the guys left with the new car, waving at the salespeople. "Goodbye, bitches!"

Mark came outside and called Freddy.

"Great job, Freddy. You proved today that you are a real salesman. That was one of those deals I haven't seen in a long time! Welcome home, Freddy!"

Everybody was now talking about Freddy. I went to congratulate him and ask how he did it. His answer was very simple. "Like I told you, you have to connect with them in the first few minutes."

"What did you tell them?"

"Oh, I told them my sister is dating Big D from Compton."

"But Freddy," I interrupted him, "you told me that you don't have a sister."

"That's exactly right. Use your imagination in order to win the customer's heart."

"I can tell you this, Freddy," I said "I will never be able to differentiate between lies and imagination."

We both started laughing.

Later that evening, Mark came in from the parking lot and made a beeline for the receptionist's desk.

"Jasmine," he said discreetly. "I want to talk to you."

"Yes sir," she said, batting her eyelashes at him. A perk of her job is that so many of the sales force were rather good-looking.

"Jasmine, there is a homeless man passed out in the alley," he said quietly. Fortunately, the showroom was less busy than usual, but he looked around. He didn't want customers to realize that he had a situation.

"I've seen him there, sir. Yes, he and another guy..." she said, but he interrupted.

"No, I've seen them, too. They hang out over in the bushes. Generally, most folks don't notice them, but that's not what I'm talking about. One of the guys, he's slumped over at the back door. Like he's ten feet away from it," he said.

She didn't say a word; she was all eyes and ears.

"And you know all the stuff that's been going on in the news," he said.

"Oh, my gosh, yes," she said. "Terrible, about the homeless guys dying in the neighborhood."

"Right," he said, "so I don't know if he's just passed-out drunk, or what. But look, I just want you to... I think you need to call 911 for me. Okay? I'm just... concerned. Plus, it does not look good for a homeless man to just be passed out at our back door. Okay? So, have the cops come, and let them handle it. Got me?" he said.

She nodded, and made the call.

The police came and determined that an ambulance was needed. They were loading Ricky into an ambulance just as I was coming in from a test drive.

I noticed the ambulance in the alley, but I had my hands full with a problem and couldn't think about what was going on there. I'd just had a tire-kicker and was a little bit frustrated. I'd spent so much time with this customer, then he wanted to leave. I had to put on a fresh face all over again, like the tears of a clown. It was all so frustrating. I didn't know how much more of this I could stand. But I did cover my ass and turned it over to Freddy just in time. Maybe he could save the sale.

Later, I heard Jasmine say, "By the way, Mark, they picked up the homeless guy."

"Oh, they arrested him?"

"No, ambulance."

"Oh, okay. Thank god he was just drunk."

"I thought he was dead," said the receptionist.

Jasmine and I clocked out at the same time as I walked her to her car.

"Did you hear about the homeless guy who was picked up today? Right behind our dealership?"

"The cops?" I asked, glad that in the dark, she could not see that I'd turned a bit pale.

"No, ambulance," she said. "I was afraid for a minute that there had been another homeless murder in the neighborhood."

"I know, that is scary. Well, hop in your car," I said, holding the door for her, "and lock yourself in," I added, feeling a little insecure about her safety in the neighborhood all of a sudden.

This was all hitting too close to home. Then my conscience was pricked.

"Why do I want to check on this guy?" I asked myself out loud. "This is crazy."

I put my keys in my pocket and walked back over to where Ricky had been staying.

"Ricky, Ricky. Are you here?" I called out, making sure no one from the dealership heard me. No one answered.

Chapter 10

The Lady in White

THE STREETLIGHT GLIMMERED on something shiny in the bushes. There was a shiny key fob on Ricky's backpack. I looked around, then reached for the bag. I looked at it for a moment.

"God. Just filthy," I said, feeling sorry for this new friend.

I looked to see if Ricky or anyone was around. I called out to him again,

"Ricky? Ricky? You here, man?"

I walked, carrying the bag under the streetlight, and decided to look inside. There was a front pocket, so I slid the zipper open. Out fell a wallet. It wasn't just any old wallet; it was an old Gucci wallet.

"That's interesting," I said to myself, and opened it.

There was Ricky's driver's license. Ricky's look is what shocked me. There was a picture of a handsome, clean-cut man. In the first plastic sleeve was a picture of a stunningly beautiful woman. Behind the plastic picture holder was a pack of credit cards. I pulled out an American Express Gold Card and than a Bank of America Visa Card, both expired.

A white business card fell out. I picked it up. On it was written, "Jason Freeman, Esq." I looked again at the driver's license picture. Something struck me about it. Maybe it was the lighting under the street lamp, but the photo reminded me of someone.

I put the wallet back in the backpack, grabbed it and took it with me. I stepped back into the dealership and discreetly stepped into a conference room, one that wasn't being cleaned by the maintenance crew. I called the number on the card. The phone rang, and a man's voice answered.

"Hello, sir, are you Jason Freeman?"

"Yes. How can I help you? It's pretty late." He sounded semi-annoyed.

"You don't know me. My name is Michael Foster, and I found your business card. Do you know a guy named Ricky Blake?"

He began talking so loudly, I had to hold the phone away from my ear. "Yes, yes, yes! Where... where is he? Is he with you? How do you know him?" The words tumbled out in a torrent.

"I think he's in the hospital," I said. "They picked him up behind the dealership where I work. I'm a salesman."

"Well, what hospital?" he asked urgently.

"I don't know," I said.

Jason said, "That's okay, I can call the police, they'll know."

Then I said, "The problem is, I found his wallet. I mean, it's not on him. You know what I mean? So, he doesn't have ID."

Jason said, "What dealership are you at? Can I come meet you there and pick up his wallet?"

"Sure, come to the dealership at Van Nuys and Burbank. I'll be out front, parked on the street in a white Toyota Camry."

"Great, I'm in a Lexus, silver. I'll be there in about twenty minutes. And thank you for calling. What is your last name again?"

"Foster," I said, "Michael Foster."

"Thank you, Michael Foster," Jason said. "You have no idea... See you in a few minutes, and thank you again."

A few minutes went by, and Jason pulled up near me and got out of his car. I walked up and I got out of my car, carrying the bag.

"You Michael?" asked Jason, his hands shaking.

"Yes. Jason?" I said, reaching out to shake Jason's hand. It was ice-cold. Jason looked like he'd seen a ghost.

"You'll have to forgive me, man. I'm a little blown away. I've called the police and located a homeless guy fitting Ricky's description admitted to Sherman Oaks hospital. That's his bag?" asked Jason.

"Yes, it is, and the wallet is inside. What's this guy's story, man?" I asked.

"It's a very long story."

"I'd like to hear," I said.

"I'm headed to the hospital," Jason said as I handed him Ricky's bag.

"Can I come with you?" I asked.

"You sure?"

"I'm very sure," I said. "I don't know why, but I want to know more about this man."

Jason said, "Hop in. I'll drop you back. Don't worry. I don't bite."

As we were buckling our seatbelts, I asked, "So what happened to him?" There was a long silence as Jason navigated our way to the hospital.

"Well... where do I start..." he said. "It's very complicated."

How to Come Back from the Dead

The story Jason told me on the way to the hospital was a tragedy no person should ever have to bear. I could see how after something so terrible, such an event could turn Ricky from the man he had been to the man I saw in the alley. People's hearts had been utterly broken beyond repair over less than this.

When we arrived at the hospital, Jason took charge and showed Ricky's picture to the reception staff at the Emergency Room, and explained who Ricky was and who he was. He was cool and efficient, every bit the top-dollar attorney, until the nurse escorted us to an examination room where Ricky lay unconscious.

Jason took one look at the man in the bed, and I thought he was going to break down. There lay a filthy man with a wild, bushy beard and hair, and with a farmer's tan. "This? This is Ricky?"

The nurse told him that this was the only John Doe they had. And I assured him that this was Ricky, the man from the alley in the back of the dealership. That was when I thought Jason would lose it entirely, but he managed to hold it together. "I promised his father…" he said, hoarse with emotion, but couldn't finish the sentence.

We stayed for as long as we could. Jason stopped in the business office on our way out, gave them his American Express Gold Card, and told them he would be responsible for all of Ricky's treatment. It was obvious that Jason truly loved Ricky. It made me think that this person I had met under such dire circumstances had once been truly lovable.

It was touch-and-go for a while as to whether or not Ricky would ever regain consciousness. But slowly, very slowly, he began to improve. I stopped by to see him a couple of times, and was there with Jason on the evening the duty nurse asked him if he knew who Isabella was. Jason didn't answer for a moment, and I could see his eyes were wet with tears. He said, "Isabella was his wife."

She had come to him again, the lady all in white. She hovered over his bed, luminous, more beautiful than anything he could have ever imagined, the kind of beauty that almost makes your heart stop, that takes your breath away and allows you to speak only in a whisper. She was floating just a few feet above him. He desperately wanted to touch her – to touch her, to be with her, to go away with her. He tried to reach out, but found that he couldn't move his hands. He was so weak, he could only lay there and watch this exquisite apparition that created such a longing in him, it almost sliced him like a knife. He thought that if he could only move his hands, he might be able to touch the hem of her garment. Her garments were made of light... of stars, clouds, mist and beauty. She was incandescent, hypnotic.

He wanted to join her, but all he could do was watch while she seemed to bedazzle him. "Ricky," he seemed to hear in his head. Her lips were not moving. She was smiling at him, a gentle, loving smile. It was as if she thought it to him, called out his name with her thoughts; and he could hear them wordlessly.

With great effort, he finally summoned the strength to raise his finger. As he caught the edge of her gown with his fingertip, she instantly transformed into a white bird – a white pigeon, and flew away into the starlight that suddenly was the ceiling of his hospital room.

"Isabella," he tried to mumble, moving his lips. Two fingers of his right hand lifted up as he tried to grasp the bird-in-flight.

The private-duty nurse Jason had hired told us later that she had heard him say the name "Isabella" and immediately pressed the button for the doctor to come.

Ricky finally regained consciousness. He'd had excellent care, and he was cleaned up. He was beginning to look just a bit like the face on his driver's license.

But it wasn't going to be a nice, happy ending, with Ricky glad to have been found. He was impatient, short-tempered, and clearly not happy to have been found at all.

A few more days passed, and Ricky was talking again. He was scheduled for his last physical therapy session, which he took no interest in; and was told that after that, the doctor would come in to release him.

He told me later what ran through his mind. "Release? To where?" But he said nothing to the nurse. He had become free as a bird, and was used to it being that way.

Then he got into a heated discussion with the nurse when he found only new clothes in the closet. All he could think about was that there had been some good stuff in the pockets that he badly wanted. When he was apprised that his attorney had thrown away the clothes he had been admitted in, he was furious.

Finally, a wheelchair was brought. He was to wait for Jason to pick him up that evening.

Ricky made his way to the closet and grabbed his back-pack. He fiddled around with it, finding the little secret hiding hole where he had put the last bit of money he and Jose hadn't squandered. It was a great spot because the bag was so dirty, no one would think any money was in it. Secondly, no one would want to stick their hand in there.

"Hello, First Bank of Ricky, Branch One!" he said, smiling to himself as he pulled out a carefully folded wad of twenties. "Andrew Jackson," he smiled, holding one of the twenties to the light. "Show me the way!" He figured out a way to hook it on the handle of his wheelchair. He slipped on his new jacket. It was very nice. He liked the smell of the leather.

Suddenly, an alarm went off, and all the nurses went to a room not far away from Ricky's. Then he just went for it. He wheeled himself out into the hallway just outside the door, then little bit more. Still no one in sight; no nurse around. He tried the wheels. Squeaking along, he was able to wheel himself a few feet, pushing the wheels of the chair with his hands. Then the elevator dinged open, and a visitor for another guest got out. There he was, right in front of an open elevator. So, he got in.

Miraculously, no one rode the elevator down with him. A family tried to get on when he was trying to get off, but they were very nice about holding the doors for him. He told me he felt that if he was going to make his exit, he better do it pretty quickly before the nurses figured out he's out.

Suddenly, he felt a cold breeze on his left shoulder and looked to his left. There was a sliding glass door, opening and closing automatically as a little girl was playing on it for fun.

Ricky managed to wheel himself out of the hospital. Just outside the visitor entrance was a taxi stand. One of them was a van. Ricky pulled up to the guy. "You next?" he said, eyeing the handicap symbol on the dash of the van.

"Yeah, where you wanna go?" asked the driver.

Ricky held up a twenty. "Will this get me to Van Nuys and Burbank?" he asked.

"Sure," said the driver, setting off the electronic van doors and hopping out of the cab. "And some change to spare," he said.

"Let's do this," said Ricky. "I'm outta this place."

They made their way down Van Nuys Boulevard from the hospital. As the taxi driver got near the dealership, Ricky looked out the window. They passed a group of people at the intersection who were preaching the word of God. They stopped at the light. An elderly man was passed out at the bus stop, cradling his forty-ounce like a newborn baby. A few blocks later, a man was sleeping on a pallet of cardboard, with a tarp covering himself and his dog watching over him for protection.

Just at that moment, Jason was walking up to the nurses' station at the hospital. He said, "I'm here to pick up my client, Ricky Blake. Do you have his discharge papers?"

The nurse said, "Sorry, we just had an emergency again today, but I do have them. I was just waiting for the doctor to speak with him before I give them to him. The doctor wants to make it very clear to him that if he goes back out and continues to abuse his body as he has in the past..." she shook her head. "He almost didn't make it this time. You can go to his room and wait with him. I will bring all the discharge papers."

Jason walked down the hall and turned the corner to Ricky's room, which was right by the elevator. The room was empty and disheveled.

Jason said, "He's not here... Where is he?"

"Oh, he must be with his physical therapist. Usually, they just walk up and down the hall together. We have to make sure he's sure on his feet," she said. So they walked around the entire floor of that wing. No Ricky. She said, "Huh, that's strange. Let's try the waiting room, maybe," she said. Still no Ricky.

Jason turned to her and said, "With all due respect, what the hell is going on?"

"I need to make a phone call," said the nurse. Just as she was picking up the phone to make a call, the physical therapist arrived at her desk.

Jason told me that's when he began to lose it. "You don't have my client? You lost my client? What in the hell is going here? What? What kind of hospital... You don't know where he is?" He knew he wasn't behaving in a businesslike, clear, lawyerly manner; but he was frustrated, angry and frightened for Ricky. And he was getting tired of trying to save him.

Nurse Smith said, "Hang on sir. Let me call the cashier's office."

They went through all the machinations of trying to locate Ricky, to no avail.

Jason, having lost his patience, said, "I hope he didn't run away from me again.

Well, I'm going to make some phone calls, too." He handed her his business card, "in case you guys do find him in the hospital." The nurse nodded and took his card.

Jason stepped away from the nurse's desk, and called George from his cell. "George, we have a problem. You remember where you saw Ricky last time, by Burbank and the 405? Please go there. It seems like he ran away from the hospital. He sneaked out, ran out, escaped, whatever you want to call it. I'm gonna go by the dealership where he was hanging out. Call me with any news."

Ricky said, "Hey, man, can you just drop me off here?"

"Not the dealership?" said the driver.

"No, here, right here on the corner," said Ricky. The driver parked the van and prepared to walk around and assist Ricky with the wheelchair lift.

Ricky said, "No, no, man, I got this." The driver stood there, astounded, when Ricky shakily stood up and got out of the van by himself. The taxi driver got the wheelchair out of the taxi, and Ricky took the handles. "You can walk?" asked the driver.

"I can walk," he said, pushing his stolen wheelchair like a walker. "Thanks, man."

Ricky walked the wheelchair to the liquor store and waited until the driver was out of sight. All of a sudden, he felt really tired. He decided the wheelchair was of good use right now, after all.

He wheeled into the store. The liquor store owner barely recognized him.

"Where you been, man?" said Ahmed.

"Just got back from a wedding," said Ricky, and they both laughed.

Ahmed pulled a quart of Black Jack from the shelf. "The usual?" he asked.

Ricky said, "Oh, you know me so well, but bring his twin brother and make it two."

"That'll put some hair on your chest," joked Ahmed.

"You know it!" laughed Ricky, handing Ahmed two twenties in exchange for the bottles.

When he got outside, he zipped one bottle in his jacket and the other in the backpack hooked on the back of his chair. He slowly wheeled himself down the alley that ran behind the liquor store to home.

When Ricky wheeled up to the area where the bushes were, he gently called out, "Jose?" But there was no answer. "The hell?" he said to himself as he looked around to see if his friend was there. He slowly extracted himself from the wheelchair, being fairly stiff from spending some days, if not weeks, in the hospital. Then he pulled the wheelchair in behind him and tucked it behind the bushes. He looked around, but no one had noticed him, so he got behind the bushes and slowly lowered himself down, as best as he could, onto the cardboard pallet he and Jose called home. "Oh, man. Gettin' old," he said to himself. What was weird was that Jose's stuff was still there.

Ricky looked, and there was the trusty old AM/FM radio. He flipped the antenna and put it on KLUV, his favorite station. Love songs came on the air. Ricky unzipped his new jacket, and pulled out the bottle of whiskey. "Ah, Jack," he said, kissing the bottle. "It looks like you are my best and only friend." He unscrewed the lid and took a long swig of the alcohol, guzzling it down like a newborn calf. Some drizzled down his chin and onto his new shirt, which he just wiped with his sleeve. "For you, Jose," he said, taking another long drink. "This is for you, Jack," he said, taking another drink, then holding up the bottle to the sky. "And this, this is for you, my Isabella," he said, taking the longest chug-a-lug of all.

Soft music began to play. Ricky began singing softly along with the music, chugging his Jack between the lyrics. He cried and drank for a while, anesthetizing himself once again to put it all behind him. Pretty soon, he began to feel like laying down, so he took his backpack and made a make-shift pillow with it. Grabbing one of Jose's tarps, he covered himself with it a little bit and laid his head down to rest for a while.

He was tired. When he lay down, he placed his hand behind his head. That's when his hand touched something cold and hard. He reached around; it felt strange in his hand. So he picked it up and held it in front of him. "A gun. Wow," he said. "Jose? What the fuck have you have gotten into?" He was thinking about the drug dealer and wondering how a gun got into their bushes.

Ricky sat up slowly again and looked at the gun for a moment. He took another swig of whiskey and said, "And this is for you, gun. Cheers." He took a better look at the pistol. ".38 special, I'd like you to meet Jack. Jack, meet our new friend, Mr. Pistol. You can just call him, .38. No, no, dirty eight... dirty eight," he said, taking another sip. "And this is for you, Jack," speaking to the bottle.

The whiskey went down hard. It burned his gullet as he swigged it. It burned the hospital bacon and eggs he had forced himself to get down his stomach that morning. It burned, and he was glad. "Burn me good, Mr. Jack," he said, "burn me good, and burn me hard. Burn my heart. Burn it all up!" He laughed, and then started to cry. "Burn it all up... burn it! Because this, this is for you, Kevin!" he said. "Because I am coming, Kevin," he cried, "you give me pain, I give you pain right back. You think you got away with this, but nooo, buddy, I got my new friend, the 'Dirty Eight,' who's gonna do me justice." He laughed cynically, holding up the revolver. "Here I come!"

Ricky took the Magnum and made one turn of the chamber. "I like the sound," he said, like a boy with a toy pistol. A dark cloud crossed Ricky's brow as his face became more serious. "And this, this is for me," he said, putting the revolver in his mouth. "I'm not going to ruin my face for you, Kevin. When my beautiful Isabella sees me again, I want her to be able to recognize me." he said, putting the revolver to his heart.

He sobbed for a second, thinking about all that he had loved and lost on this earth. He saw flashes of his entire life with Isabella, from the first time he saw her, and all their wonderful times together — dinner, at the beach, her art, the first time they'd made love, the first dance at their wedding when he felt as though he was the luckiest man on Earth to have this splendid woman as his wife. He saw his parents and hers, almost as happy as they were, and he saw the house they were designing together, in his mind built and beautiful, the house where they were to spend their lives together and raise their unborn children, where they would have friends to dinner, where they would celebrate all of life's milestones. He thought he could hear that marvelous husky laugh of hers that always seemed to turn him on.

And how there was nothing, less than nothing because part of his heart was gone, hollowed out and empty. There was no one here for him; that world, his world, was an empty place, as empty as his heart.

He pointed the revolver to his chest, digging it into his solar plexus. His hands were shaking, and he shut his eyes hard. "I'm coming, Kevin. You better run!" he said. "See you in hell!"

He pulled the trigger.

"Click." The gun's chamber made a turn. Nothing happened. Ricky opened his eyes and looked at the gun. "What the? Really?" he exclaimed, looking at the idiocy of the gun. Ricky was so angry and so frustrated. The situation was so ridiculous. Now, he was furious, but this also made him more determined than ever.

Chapter 11

The Only Way Out is Through

I WAS COMING out of the dealership. When I got to the alley, I opened my paycheck. I could not believe my eyes. "Fuck!" I said to myself. "Fuck your meetings, big-shot manager, with your fucking cocksucker friends." I walked toward my car and turned around the corner.

I thought I heard Ricky's voice. I walked towards the wall and looked inside the encampment. The sight that met my eyes shocked me. There was Ricky, sitting with a gun, opening the chamber. He was counting bullets. "One, two, you little bastards," he said. Ricky closed the revolver. He prepared to shoot.

Instinctively, I jumped over the low wall between us. Just as Ricky was going to pull the trigger again, my reflexes took over. I didn't think, I didn't hesitate; I just acted. I grabbed Ricky's wrist and wrested the gun from his hand.

Ricky sat there in shock for a moment. Then, it started to drizzle, as if someone or something had cued the sky.

Jason pulled to a screeching halt, and hopped out of his car, the engine still running. He hoped to find Ricky where I had told him he'd been camping out. He found more than he bargained for.

"What the hell is going on?" he said, looking at the two of us in the alley.

The drizzle turned to rain, and the drops merged with the tears that began to stream down Ricky's face.

I was showing Ricky my garage-conversion apartment. I shrugged it off as just something one human being would do for another.

"This is your bed. It's a futon, it opens. There's your TV, the bathroom's through there. I'm going to go make us a couple of sandwiches, and I'll be right back."

I went to my kitchen to make the sandwiches. Elaine, my wife, was there, sitting and waiting for me. "Honey, what are you doing? You're bringing a stranger into our home, and you don't even ask me?"

"Please, please, trust me. I said it's gonna be temporary."

"I do trust you. But honey?"

It was going to take time. I knew that. It would take time and a great deal of patience. My wife said, "Just for a few weeks, OK?" I pointed skyward and said, "We'll see."

When I went back to the garage apartment with sandwiches and fresh lemonade, Ricky was still standing awkwardly with his suitcase in his hand.

"Hey, Ricky, put the stuff down and relax. Take it easy. Consider this your home for now. And don't make me eat alone."

Slowly, Ricky put the bag down, uncertain, still feeling bewildered as to why anyone would do this for him. He didn't feel deserving. In fact, he felt totally undeserving. But he sat down with me at the little table. It was the first time he had sat down at a table to eat with anyone in a very long time. He felt strange and tentative. It would have surprised me to know how confident and self-assured this fragile and withdrawn man had once been.

We were just beginning to eat when Jason pulled up in his Lexus, followed by George in his SUV.

"Well, dig in, man!" I said.

George was baffled, and thought it was a very strange turn of events. Jason was adamantly opposed to the idea of Ricky staying with us. He was here to talk some sense into us.

He rang the doorbell. I excused myself, telling Ricky I'd be right back, and met them outside the front door. I knew they were coming and that Jason probably had things to say that Ricky shouldn't hear right at this moment. I thought he shouldn't hear anything negative, or have any kind of conflict.

Elaine went off to see to our daughters. She was feeling less than comfortable with a strange man in her home, at night no less. I was relieved. If Jason was going to mount a case against Ricky being here in our home, I didn't really want Elaine to hear it as she might well agree with him.

Jason cut right to the chase. "Can we talk?"

"Sure," I said.

George asked, "Well, what we want to say, is... What we want to ask is... Are you... Are you sure?"

Jason cut him off. "This is a terrible idea. He belongs in rehab as an inpatient, not outpatient. I can have him committed. He's a danger to himself. That's enough for seventy-two hours. After that, we can..."

"Hold on, hold on, hold on. Let's just try this. Rehab hasn't worked for him. Let's give him a real home and see how that works. My wife is an amazing cook, a whole lot better than what he'd get in any institution. We'll get a little weight on him. Let me... let us. Give him a little space. Just give him some time, some normal family time."

"As his attorney, I don't agree."

"Okay. I know you don't, Jason, but does Ricky have a choice in the matter?"

Looking back, I am surprised at how determined I was. There was something driving me to shield Ricky from any stress... Anything that could upset him in the state he was in.

"Does he have a choice in the matter?" repeated Jason.

"He does have a choice in the matter, doesn't he?" asked George.

"Not if I say he doesn't." Jason was ever the lawyer, but I knew he loved Ricky and was afraid he'd lose him again. His opposition came from love.

"Why is that?" I asked.

"Because the man tried to kill himself, that's why, and he's run away from rehab and me and the hospital. It's too much. Because he is a danger to himself and others. That's why. Did we all just suddenly forget he was about the pull the trigger when you..."

"You turned the gun in, right?"

Jason nodded. He had tuned the weapon over to the authorities.

"Okay, no gun, then. Look, I've seen him in the hospital and in rehab. I didn't see a change. He will still go to rehab, but I just think he really needs more than just medications and supervision. If I see any signs at all that this isn't working, I will contact you immediately and we'll insist that he do inpatient rehab. But I really believe we're going to be okay. Don't ask me why I believe this. It's just a feeling I have in my bones."

"Are you sure?" George was less opposed than Jason.

"He was suicidal. I don't think he's homicidal," I said.

The men could see Ricky through the converted garage window.

"If you're sure, man," said Jason, shaking his head. He wasn't sure why I was taking Ricky into my home, and I don't think I could have really explained it at that moment.

"I am." I responded, sounding more certain than I might have been.

George dropped Ricky off at Valley Recovery Center for his session. "We are here, Ricky," George said.

Ricky was looking through car window at the parking lot, where this young blonde lady was arguing with her companion, a much older guy, the driver. She shut the car door, hard.

She said, "Leave me alone!"

The man said, "Okay, I will see you here in the parking lot, same spot."

"Who cares?" she said, walking away angrily.

Ricky said, "Thanks, man."

George said, "Don't forget, Ricky. Michael is going to pick you up at five."

"I know."

Ricky walked toward the main entrance for his rehab. As he approached, his eyes connected with the beautiful blonde. "You can tell she's been through hell," he thought to himself. She had a lot of makeup on, trying to cover a black eye.

He got the door for her.

"After you," he said. She was still angry, but his gentility broke through her façade a little, and she smiled.

"You work here?" she asked him.

Ricky said, "Just the program."

"Ah," she said, as they walked down the hallway together to go sign in. "Me, too." She signed in for the group that afternoon, and then smiled as she handed him the pen to sign in. Ricky signed in, then handed the clipboard back to the lady behind the front desk. "I'm Vanessa," she said.

"Pleased to meet you, Vanessa," he said, "I'm Ricky." He held out his hand to shake hers, but when they shook, he held on to her fingers just a little too long. She began walking toward their classroom, and he followed along.

"Well, this is me," she said.

"It's me, too," Ricky said.

"Oh!" said Vanessa, smiling at him.

The other participants were already seated, and the counselor came in, "Hi, I'm Samuel. Welcome."

After the session they walked together to the parking lot.

"Do you have a cigarette?" she asked.

"No, sorry, I quit yesterday," he joked, and she smiled.

"Do you have Mr. Samuel every week?"

"No, I usually have Mr. Jordan," she said, "but I think I'm going to ask for Mr. Samuel from now on."

"Yeah!"

"He's really good," said Vanessa.

"Yeah, he really got me when he said, 'Treat the problem, rather than the symptom. It made me think for a moment.'"

Vanessa laughed a little, "Yeah, I didn't quite get that, but then again, I'm new."

"Well, I haven't been here that long myself, but that phrase really resonated with me." Then Vanessa's ride came to pick her up.

Ricky later told me he thought she was beautiful, and wondered how she got that shiner.

I drove up at the same time Vanessa was leaving, and told Ricky to hop in. I had to go pick up my daughters. Ricky got in but didn't say anything. I thought I saw an imperceptible grin on his face. We rode in silence. I didn't make him speak unless he wanted to. I didn't want to press him or anything. He'd been so wounded. He needed peace, not pressure. He was looking out the window and was actually smiling, something I'd never seen him do before.

"Whatever put that smile on your face, I think it's awesome," I told him.

"What are you talking about?" Ricky laughed a little, like I'd caught him with something. "It's nothing."

"It's just nice seeing you smile. I don't think I've seen much of that." I decided to tease him just a little bit. "So, this nothing, is she blonde, brunette, redhead?" He told me to shut up, but he was still smiling.

We pulled up to the piano teacher's house, and I went up to the door to retrieve the kids. I opened the doors for them, but it was Ricky who made sure their seatbelts were fastened well. I think my daughters were like a tonic for him. When he was with them, I believe his heart was a little lighter.

"Hi, Mr. Ricky!" said Stephanie.

"Hi, Mr. Ricky!" said Alexandra.

"Hi, girls." They were so adorable. "How was piano?"

"Mrs. Stevens has bad breath!" said Stephanie, my younger one.

I told them that wasn't nice of them.

"But it's true," said Alexandra, "for real! Maybe it's not nice of her to have bad breath, but her breath smells like throw-up!"

Ricky just burst out laughing. "You know what you should do?" he asked. "The next time you're over, have a box of mints and accidentally leave it there."

"That's a very good idea, Uncle Ricky," I agreed. "We'll do that." Ricky smiled and looked out the window again.

When we got home, the girls ran in to see their mother, as they always did. I grabbed their backpacks and handed one to Ricky. "Jesus, these things are heavy." He was surprised that two small girls carried these things around every day.

"You have no idea. These books… the kids have to alternate shoulders when they carry them to avoid spine problems. It's crazy."

Ricky was silent. There was so much he didn't know, so much he missed. If he'd become a father. he would know these things. As I walked into the house, Ricky stood back a little and just took in the whole house, the whole family thing. This is what he might have had.

"C'mon in. Don't be late for dinner, or Elaine will serve my head on a platter."

Ricky dropped the backpack, and one of the girls came and hugged him, and said, "Look, Mr. Ricky, I made this for you in school!" and handed him a picture. It was a drawing of a man; on it was a wheel of cut-out pictures from a magazine that surrounded his head. "You think about a lot of things!" she said, pointing to a picture of a car wheel that was glued on the drawing. "I made this, because this is you!" she said.

Ricky smiled and patted her on her head.

"It's beautiful. I will treasure it." And in truth, he was deeply touched.

Elaine called the girls to get washed up for dinner – school uniforms changed and homework finished. Gently, she told Ricky to spruce himself up a little as we were having company. "Grandma and Grandpa are coming, and Uncle George," she told the girls. "C'mon!"

"Listen to mom," said Ricky, "I'm sure it's going to be just fine." He took the picture that Alexandra had made for him and headed toward the garage apartment. He taped it on his minibar fridge, looked at it and thought "Boy, she really has my number."

He told me later he went into his tiny bathroom and splashed some water on his face. When he was drying his face with the towel, he caught a true glimpse of his face in the mirror. He pulled up close to the mirror, and then back again. He studied the reflection carefully. "I look… Better," he thought, and realized he looked more like himself than he had in a very, very long time. And maybe – just maybe – he was beginning to care just a little. He was still studying his image when he heard me calling.

"Dinner!"

"Coming!"

The girls began to argue about who was going to sit next to Ricky. He realized that it pleased him to know that these darling children liked him. He hadn't cared about himself or anyone else for so long. He sat between the two of them. "How about this?"

"Yay!" He made them very happy with his solution.

The front doorbell rang. "I got it," I said. I knew who it was.

"Hey, hey! Where are my girls?" my father bellowed. The girls ran to him, and hugged him. Stephanie, the littlest one, wrapped herself around his leg, so then he had to walk to the table with a little girl attached.

Alexandra wrapped her arms around my mother. "My Mee-boo!"

"Wait, wait!" said Grandma Mimi, "You'll spill the casserole," she smiled.

"Elaine," said Grandpa Bill. "Look! I have a little sea urchin attached to my leg."

"C'mon, girls," Elaine said, kissing Grandpa Bill and Grandma Mimi each on the cheek. "You're going to cause an accident. Scoot, scoot! Into your seats! There you go!" she shepherded the kids. There was so much love in the house. I thought it had to be good for Ricky, or at least I hoped it would be, and not just a reminder of everything he'd lost.

"Who's the handsome young man?" Mimi asked Elaine.

"That's Uncle Ricky!" said Alexandra.

"Yes!" said Stephanie.

"Pleased to meet you, Uncle Ricky," Grandma Mimi said, her eyes twinkling.

Ricky said, "I'm so glad to meet you. I'm Ricky Blake."

Grandpa Bill said, "Very nice to meet you. How do you know Michael?"

"Oooohhh, that's a long story!" Elaine interjected quickly. "Mama, will you help me in the kitchen for a minute?"

"Sure, dear!"

The doorbell rang again. I was relieved that there would be no lengthy explanations. "That must be George. I'll get it!"

George entered, his usual larger-than-life self. He handed me a bottle of wine, "For you, brother," he said. He walked into the kitchen with some flowers for Elaine. "These are for the lovely lady of the house."

"Oh, George. They're beautiful, thank you! You always bring flowers; you don't have to!" she smiled, loving them. "Mom, let's get these in water!"

"You didn't tell me your beautiful sister was going to be here," he said, scooping up my mother in a bear hug.

"Oh, you," Grandma Mimi said, laughing as she play-slapped at his embrace.

Grandpa Bill stood up and went over and shook George's hand.

"Unhand my woman, sir," he joked.

"You didn't tell me about your boyfriend. Do we have to duel?"

"You guys!" My mother was actually blushing as she straightening her blouse.

Ricky was studying the domestic scene, the humor and play and love and warmth between all of them. It was something he might have had, something he had wanted, and he realized it was the warmth that he missed most. He had felt so cold, almost frozen, for so long.

"Ahem! I need everyone to take their seats, please. I can't get food to the table. I love you all but move!" Elaine smiled.

George looked at Ricky seated between the two girls. "What, I don't get to sit next to the princesses?"

"Hi, Uncle George!" said the girls.

"Hold out your hands and close your eyes, and you will get a big surprise!" George said. He reached into his pocket and pulled out two tiny pink stuffed kittens on keychains. "Okay, open!" he said.

"Ooooh!" my daughters were delighted with his gifts.

"For your backpacks." Stephanie smiled and twirled the little kitten around and around on her finger, smiling. Alexandra kissed hers.

"Sayyyy... Ricky!" said George, reaching across the table to try and high-five Ricky. Ricky high-fived him back, just going with the flow.

The ladies came to the table bearing dinner.

"Dinner is served, everyone," Elaine said as she placed dishes on the table, as did Grandma Mimi. "Thank you, God, for letting us gather here at this table. Amen!" she said and simultaneous the rest of us said "Amen".

I poured wine for some, water for others. Then everyone enjoyed the meal.

"Mmm, delicious!" said George, taking a bite. "A single guy doesn't get a home-cooked meal every day."

"Delicious, huh, *Guapo*?" George asked Ricky. Ricky's face turned crimson, but he didn't say anything. He loved George's larger-than-life presence, but it was a lot for him to take in with his nerves still so raw.

"What's *guapo,* Daddy?" Stephanie asked.

"Uh, it means good-looking in Spanish," Elaine answered, smiling at Ricky.

"Uncle *Guapo!*" said Alexandra.

"So, when are you gonna make me a godfather?" said George in between munching on salad. Ricky couldn't help himself; his face fell a little. George carried on with his jovial conversation. His intentions were always good. The guy didn't have a malicious bone in his body. But he wanted the old Ricky back so badly, he sometimes missed the effect he had on his friend.

It was a lovely dinner, as it always was when we all got together, laughing and teasing with stories and love. I looked at my family and I thought, "I hate my job, but look what I have here; everything that Ricky lost. I am one lucky son of a bitch."

Ricky hardly said a word at dinner, but everyone was enjoying the food and the company so much, they didn't quite notice. He couldn't help himself. He was missing so much. He was missing his parents, and Isabella, and the unborn children they would never have. Her parents and his would never be grandparents. And right now, he hated George for being so damn happy. He just wanted to eat and get out of there. What he really wanted was a drink. And more than that, he wanted to just get fucked up. When he was done, he could politely excuse himself and head toward his apartment and be alone with silence.

When he did just that, George immediately said, "Hey man, you're not going to your place already?"

Ricky just looked at him and said quietly, "Yeah, man, I'm just... I'm just really tired."

"You're a party-pooper," said George.

"Aren't you going to stay for dessert?" Elaine asked.

"No, but thank you so much," said Ricky, patting his belly. "I'm just stuffed," he said. It was true. But moreover, he was despondent and angry and frustrated, wanting more than anything on Earth to use. However, he couldn't let on to them that he felt as though he was tailspinning out into oblivion, that he was in trouble. No, because someone would surely get in the way of his addiction. Someone would surely call Jason. And Ricky had a date: he had a date with his addiction. That monkey was on his back.

Grandpa Bill said, "Yeah, would you look at the time? It is getting really late."

"Oh, no. Do you really have to go?" I asked.

Elaine said, "C'mon girls, let's get you ready for bed."

I got up and started clearing dishes, and George helped me. George turned to see that Ricky was no longer there. He had noticed Ricky's mood darken throughout the meal. "Did I do something wrong?" he asked me.

"No, but... We really have to just give him his space," I said. "He's walking around like he has no skin on his body and all his nerves are exposed. Sometimes, he needs quiet and space more than he needs us trying to cheer him up. Just give it time, George... Just time."

Chapter 12

Redemption

T HEY SAY TIME heals all wounds. I'm not sure that's entirely true. But while wounds may never totally heal, yes, time makes them less painful. Somehow, you can live again. Somehow, you can move forward. I just had the feeling that if Ricky could stay sober long enough and begin slowly to build a life, even his acute pain could at least be salved.

Though at first, I wasn't sure if he was even sane. In the hospital, he had kept mumbling about a pigeon that was really a woman made of light and spoke to him without words. Maybe all the alcohol and drugs had damaged his brain. Why I chose to be the one to help him rebuild, chose to bring a homeless drug-addicted drunk into my home, I can't really articulate, even to myself. Of course, it had something to do with my brother, but it was more than that. There was just something about him that made me want to know him, especially after Jason had told me what had happened to him. It was such an unspeakably terrible loss.

Elaine was horrified at first and worried about our children, and thought *I* was the one who had lost his mind. But when I explained, as best I could, how important it was to me, she looked at me for a long time, as if she was trying to see this through my eyes, then embraced me so very tenderly, in a way she hadn't for a long time, the way she had before children and bills and the vicissitudes of life had begun to weigh on us. She whispered, "Do whatever you need to do, Michael."

When I sift through my memories, I think it was the look in Ricky's eyes that made me open my home to him. I don't believe I knew it consciously then, but my subconscious recognized that look as the same as that I had seen in my brother's eyes. I couldn't save Chris, and I believe that will haunt me forever, but maybe – just maybe – I could help this man who had endured such pain and tragedy.

I knew that our scenes of domestic warmth, closeness and family were like a double-edged sword for Ricky. On the one hand, he had peace and affection here with me Elaine, who had become quite fond of Ricky and had forgotten about her two-week limit, and our daughters, who were sweet and funny with him. And that was healing. On the other hand, these scenes were a painful reminder of all that he had lost.

Sometimes we just needed to give him some breathing room to work through things on his own.

I also knew that he wouldn't want to live in a garage apartment forever. He had been a man of means – the 'Malibu Guy' – who had lived well and was accustomed to fine things and who had, from what I gathered from George, excellent, discerning taste. It was hard to imagine him wanting to sleep on a futon indefinitely.

It was later, after everyone had left, probably around midnight, when I went down to the kitchen to have some leftover pie and decided to take out the trash. I noticed a light on in Ricky's room. I thought I'd look in on him for a moment, just to see if he was going through a bad moment.

I opened his door and asked him if he was all right. But instead of answering me, he just said, "I saw it." He appeared to be almost in a trance. I had no idea what he meant; but it seemed vitally, urgently important to him, so I tried to understand. I put my hand on his shoulder and asked him what he'd seen. He told me he'd seen the white pigeon again. I was confused. I asked him if a bird had gotten into the room. He just repeated that he'd seen the same white pigeon, and I could see that something internal was working on him. I was having a difficult time discerning what this could mean, but I didn't say a word.

"You don't understand. There's a pigeon – a white pigeon," Ricky said.

"OK, Rick, a white pigeon. What does that mean to you?"

"It's the white pigeon… The one that follows me everywhere."

"It does?"

"Yes... But this time, I had the chance to talk to it again."

"You... You spoke to..."

Before I could finish my sentence, he said, "Yes, and I know now, it came to check up on me... To see how I was doing."

"You have a pigeon that checks up on you?"

"Yeah, yeah, I do. It was *her*! I know you think I'm losing it again, but I'm telling you this is real. It was my Isabella. She was checking on me... To.. To see... To see if I'm OK. I know it was her." He smiled at me with his eyes full of tears, and he hugged me!

I looked at him. I could see that whatever this was, it was soothing him... Something my brother didn't have. And who was I to take that away from him? I just smiled at him and said, "I believe in angels too, Ricky."

I knew that when I picked Ricky up from his meetings at the rehab center that he always looked a little less tense, as though his spirit that had been so utterly and completely devastated had somehow been lifted. George and Jason noticed it when they picked him up as well. And I could see that it was the blonde, Vanessa, who seemed to be able to even make him smile more. But I was dubious about it all. I thought it was much too soon, and moving too fast. I'd known enough guys who had been in AA to know that they tell you not to get involved in a relationship until you've had at least a full year of recovery, clean and sober. It absolutely made sense. You're fragile; you need time to get your head straight.

I have to admit I was really worried. But Ricky was a grown man, and I couldn't dictate to him. I could only give him a safe, quiet place and hope that, along with his meetings, that would be enough.

So on the day that Ricky invited Vanessa to visit him for the first time, I was both hopeful that this would not interfere with his recovery and watchful for anything I thought might hurt him. I felt very protective toward him. The light he had in his eyes while waiting for her to arrive was something I would have given anything to see in Chris's eyes, and I vowed to myself I would not let Ricky see any of the doubt I felt.

He was nervous. He had cleaned the garage apartment so thoroughly, I didn't think I'd ever seen it so immaculate. Even Elaine was impressed, and she sets a very high bar. He'd sprayed air freshener. He showered and shaved, not a hair out of place. Elaine pointed out that he had actually styled it, which I don't think I would ever have noticed.

I could see the driveway from my kitchen window. Vanessa's father dropped her off, and as she was walking up the path to the house, I heard her father yell out the window, "Tell him if he lays one hand on you, he is a dead man." I think he had the same doubts I did, and who could blame him?

She yelled back at him, "Quiet, dad! My god!" She was shushing and laughing as he drove off. She was a beauty. She wore a yellow sundress with a daisy pattern. In her hands, she held a bunch of daisies, with one behind her ear. Elaine and I laughed at each other because we were acting like two old spinsters peeking out from between the curtains. We couldn't help it. We both felt we had a proprietary interest in Ricky, and we were anxious about anything that could potentially harm him.

We saw Ricky come out to greet her. She handed him the flowers and said, "For you."

He smiled and told her that no one had ever given him flowers before. Then they went inside Ricky's apartment. Elaine and I stepped away from the window. We couldn't watch over him anymore. What would be, would be.

The story he told me later made us both happy for him, and I was even less concerned than I had been before. They'd had a wonderful time together. They had played at being British: Ricky the butler and Vanessa the lady. He served her sandwiches and salads from a local market, and poured iced tea into her glass from a pitcher that Elaine had thoughtfully made for him. He told her his story, and I was afraid that might change their course, but she was strong enough to tell him, "We all have our own cross to bear." They had kissed, but when they had become passionate, she began to cry. He told her he wanted to protect and shield her from pain. I thought, but didn't say aloud, "Jesus, Ricky, you're still on pretty shaky ground yourself. How are you going to take this on now?"

She had a lover named Mark, who had been killed by his supplier. He met his suppliers in a downtown motel. He didn't have the money he owed them, but he wanted to tell them he would get it. Vanessa had gone with him because the fool didn't think they'd harm him in front of her. He had been dealing for them; and they wanted their nine thousand dollars, money he definitely didn't have. They slit his throat right in front of her, and he bled out on the floor. Then they took their turns with her all night long in that filthy motel room. Then they sold her to anyone who could pay. For a week, she was at their mercy in that terrible place, with strangers pawing at her body. Between the terrible rapes with strangers, they beat her and used her until Mark's debt was paid off. Then they left her to die at the Sepulveda Dam. Had it not been for the dog of a jogger finding her, she would have died. She had been deeply ashamed and cried inconsolably as she tried to tell Ricky what had happened to her.

As I listened to Ricky telling me all of this, I thought, "Oh my god, they are two deeply, incredibly damaged people." What she had lived through was horrible. It had to have left a terrible mark on her psyche. I was very much afraid that neither were strong enough to build any kind of real relationship and sustain it. I wanted to step in and intervene and tell Ricky to slow down, but I knew I couldn't. If I didn't know it myself, Elaine was there to remind me to let Ricky heal on his own terms. If he didn't, I had done the best I could. Now, when I reflect on it, I realize that so much of that fear was about my brother, Chris.

As I watched their relationship grow, I could see that in many ways, Vanessa was good for him. He looked a little better, but his body had taken a real beating. Living on the streets had taken its toll, and it would be a while before that abuse could be reversed. But Vanessa got him to exercise. She loved hiking and being outdoors, something she'd somehow managed to maintain even through her drinking and drugging days. He'd been pretty sedentary, disappearing into the apartment and watching television for hours whenever he wasn't with us or with her. But she got him to go outside. She teased and cajoled gently until she got him to start walking the hills with her. He tired easily at first, but little by little, he gained stamina; it seemed to me that he was proud of the progress he was making.

They were out taking a walk around the neighborhood when he saw a house for sale. Vanessa thought he was stopping because he couldn't keep up, but when she turned to chastise him, she saw that he was looking at a house. She asked him if he was house-shopping, and he asked her, "With what money?" She then began to encourage him to go back to his work.

I knew that one of his friends – someone who had been at his wedding – had given Ricky his business card and told him his brokerage was a little shorthanded. I had said nothing when he told me. I knew he needed to work, not so much for the money, although he needed that, as for his own well-being. I wasn't sure he could take the pressure, but Vanessa was insistent. She worked in wardrobe on a cable series, and she knew that working was better than isolating oneself in front of a television screen. And so, she pushed.

As time passed, I began to trust her. As she recovered, Elaine and I began to see the person Vanessa had been before addiction took hold of her. She had lived through the horrible, devastating experience that Ricky had related to me. She was sunny and playful and smart and kind and funny with my daughters, and always brought them little gifts. I had to admit that she was giving Ricky love and support, and those things helped him heal. As I drove by them one day on my way home, I saw them standing in front of a house for sale. I heard Ricky yell at the top of his voice, "I love this woman, did you know that?" Mrs. Franklin, an elderly neighbor who was sweeping her front porch, said, "Yes, yes, good for you."

A couple of months later, Elaine and I were in bed watching something on TV. It was about 10:30, I think, when Elaine said she heard the doorbell. I went and opened the door, and there was Vanessa with a box in her hand and Ricky standing beside her. She just said, "Surprise! God, I hope we didn't wake you." I told her they hadn't. We were just watching TV. Ricky said they just wanted to thank us for everything we had done for both of them. She said we were lifesavers. That was not the way I thought of myself at all.

They had brought a cake and a beautiful orchid. It was such a sweet gesture. Here were these two fragile people who had been through hell and back, working so hard to find their strength again. In part, they seemed to have found it in one another. It seemed so important to them to express their gratitude. I would have stopped them from heaping praise on Elaine and me; but somehow, I just knew this was something they needed to do, even if I felt both self-conscious and un-deserving.

Elaine made coffee, and we enjoyed the cake together. Who cared what time it was? Vanessa asked us to leave a few slices for the girls. It seemed so normal and ordinary and wonderful, like four old friends just talking and enjoying one another's company.

Then Vanessa began asking a question, but hesitated and asked that I forgive her if she was asking something too private. I told her she could ask me anything. And so, she did. She asked me why I had done all this for Ricky.

I answered, "That's a very long story. Are you sure you want to know?" I asked because I wasn't sure I wanted to tell it. I was stalling, playing for time to collect my thoughts. But they both asked me to go on.

"Well, I had a brother. I had an amazing brother. Great-looking, seemed to get great grades without even trying. He was a star athlete, a leader, a brave soldier with commendations. But something happened when he came back... I don't know. Something. Maybe undiagnosed untreated PTSD. He was so different... Not himself. And me and my mother and father, our friends... We didn't know how to help him. Maybe if I knew then some of what I know now... Maybe... Maybe... He was just not Chris... Just different."

Ricky asked how he was different.

"Darker, withdrawn, short-tempered, easily distracted... Just not himself. You sure you want to hear the rest?" They encouraged me to continue.

"OK, let me start from the beginning. He was always the leader of the pack when we were young; all our friends looked up to him. He was the star quarterback. But when he came back from Afghanistan, especially after his second tour, he was like a ghost... Just a shell of what he'd been. Prior to this, he had won the lottery – big time. He had real money for the first time in his life. The local news covered the story. His face was everywhere for several days.

"Then he met a girl. She had sized him up and knew he was the winner when she approached him in a bar. I was there. I saw it. They got really serious, really fast, and he married her. But she was so wrong for him... Just wrong... The wrong sort, you know? And that's when I think the real trouble began." The words were just tumbling out, I couldn't have stopped myself then. I hardly knew the others were there listening. "I think she was always cheating on him. She seemed to go out of her way to make him crazy... To make him jealous. He had beautiful kids and a great house, but she never let him feel at ease and comfortable. Every time they had a party – and they gave parties all the time because that's what she wanted – she was flirting with any man who was or was not attached." Elaine was looking at me as though she was concerned, but I was beyond the point where anything could have stopped me.

"We didn't know much of this at the time. From the outside, everything looked great. I said, gorgeous house, gorgeous kids, gorgeous life... The American dream... But no. Then out of the blue, one day, Cynthia... That was her name... Calls my mother and tells her she's kicked Chris out of the house. He's been sleeping at a hotel for a month... He's a bum... She has a restraining order against him for domestic violence, all this stuff that was terrible for my mother to hear. She even swore at my mother. Jesus, she was a lowlife.

"I wanted to confront him and ask him why he hadn't said anything to any of us. But I thought maybe that would be too painful for him, so we decided to have a barbecue and invite him. Elaine and I invited him to come stay with us, told him he was welcome any time.

"I took him aside at the barbecue. We had a couple of drinks together, and he admitted to me that Cynthia had filed for divorce and taken custody of the kids. When he accepted the invitation to come stay with us, I thought everything would be OK... That he just needed place to regroup. He told me it would take him a couple of days to get everything of his out of Cynthia's house. But we knew he was angry, too.. I think he felt disgraced. I'd never seen him that angry. Elaine and I kind of cooled him down a little bit. We served him great food. Mom and dad hugged him... A lot. By the time he left, he seemed to be in good spirits, and we were happy he had consented to stay with us. We thought he will be just fine... A hundred percent."

I had to stop for a moment and compose myself. I had never sat down and told the story this way before. It wasn't easy; in fact, it was very painful. But I looked at the two people sitting across from me and I thought, "If they could walk into a room full of strangers and tell their stories, truly tragic as they were, I could tell mine to two people I cared about."

"The next morning, mom found some flowers at their door. She called me and asked if I had left them, and I told her no. There was no card, but somehow, I... I got a chill up my spine. Sometimes, you know things before you know them... 'Ya know what I mean? I didn't really understand what had happened, but I had a bad feeling." I stopped for a moment to take a breath. I didn't want to come undone. Elaine must have seen it because she put her hand on my shoulder and just pressed gently.

"Then what happened was," I cleared my throat and tried to hold back my tears before I continued, "He… He was in the parking lot of a nearby park, and he had a… Bottle of whiskey in his hand. He was dialing and dialing, sitting there in that car alone with that bottle of whiskey… He was dialing… He was calling his kids, but no one picked up. Then the answering machine started with the voices of those sweet kids…"

Vanessa asked very softly if Chris had left a message.

"Yeah… He did. On his last call, as he was hanging up, he just said, 'This time, I'm leaving for real,' and hung up." I didn't even realize that I was crying when I continued.

"The cops found him in the parking lot the next morning in his car, with a gunshot to his heart."

There was a stunned silence when I finished. I could see they were all crying with me. Then Ricky said, "And when you saw me with the gun and the whiskey…" He didn't have to finish the sentence. He just said, "I am so sorry, man."

"Yeah, I knew what was coming next when I saw you there. I knew. And I would be goddamned if I'd let it happen again. I was going to talk to this man. This time, I would have the chance." And we were a mess, all four of us, sitting at that table and crying. "So… So, that's why I invited Ricky to come home with me."

I'd never told anyone the whole story, as I did that late night in the kitchen… Never like that. I was always afraid I would break down, which I did, but it was cathartic. I couldn't bring Chris back. I'd lost my brother, but I had gained a true friend. Ricky smiled at me and grabbed my arm in a forearm lock, and I knew then I would never lose him.

Vanessa opened the door to their new apartment and welcomed us. It was the first time Elaine and I had seen their new home. My mother and father, always delighted to have our daughters with them, and our daughters always happy to stay with their grandparents who indulged them shamelessly, had given us a night to ourselves.

Elaine and I brought Ricky and Vanessa a housewarming gift. I heard someone behind me say, "Hey, nice place," and turned to see that they had invited George, and behind him, Jason and his wife. I think I joked about not letting riff-raff in. I was feeling good.

Their new place was nicely done. Ricky had a nice inheritance, enough to help him get back on his feet. His old friend, Kazuki, had welcomed him into his real estate brokerage.

Ricky had rekindled his friendships with his entire old crowd, every one of whom had been truly happy when he reached out to them. They were all there that night. Some of them would become my friends, too.

He had ordered Hot Wings, Subway and Veggie Dips and urged everyone to dig in. I looked around the room and I could see that all these people were here because every one of them was truly happy to have their friend back. I could see enough... Just enough... Of the confident man Ricky had been. It was evident that he had been the kingpin in this crowd, just as my brother had long ago been the golden boy of his circle of friends.

Ricky made a little speech about how he and Vanessa wanted to share their new apartment with their friends, and Vanessa thanked everyone for their gifts. Both Ricky and Vanessa looked so healthy and fit, it was almost impossible to imagine the depths they had come from. The man I had seen in the hospital looked at least twenty years older than the Ricky I saw before me. His skin had been mottled and hung on him like an oversized garment; and his eyes had been dead, his face a mask of grief. The man I observed now was handsome, energetic, quick, very witty, and almost playful. He went round the room and thanked each and every one of his friends for not giving up on him, for searching for him, Jason for his loyalty and for keeping his affairs in order and his wife for putting up with his craziness, George for his sense of humor and always making him laugh, Kazuki for welcoming him into his real estate brokerage and helping him get back on his feet. Then he said, "Last, but most definitely not least, I want to thank my brother. I was not given a brother by birth, but I was given a brother by heart, indeed. Michael, thank you for saving my life."

I knew if I spoke I would lose it, so I just nodded. Ricky just said, "Get over here," and enveloped me a bear hug. With one arm still around my shoulders, he reminded everyone that they had a reservation at the Blue Moon in thirty minutes. We were all to meet there.

On the drive there, I thanked Elaine for her trust in me and allowing me to bring a filthy homeless man into our home.

She just said, "Stop, you'll make me cry. And you, my love, because of that big heart of yours, we have wonderful new friends, so you gave me a gift."

When we arrived at the Blue Moon, we were escorted to a small private dining room with a beautiful ocean view. There were wonderful desserts on the tables and champagne. After we had all helped ourselves and everyone was feeling celebratory, Ricky and Vanessa asked us all to give them a few minutes, and then to follow them outside.

As they walked from the Blue Moon's back door toward the ocean, Vanessa took Ricky's elbow. They walked together down the boardwalk. I remember that night so vividly. It was twilight. There were a few lingering clouds from a recent rainstorm. They were lit up by the sunset in streaks of orange and purple, magenta and silver. A perfect crescent moon was rising, and a few stars glimmered here and there. The ocean was lit up by the lavender and gold of the sunset, and the whole horizon was an impressionist painting awash in lilac and peach pastels, as though an artist had smudged just a little so that everything was soft and it seemed you could hardly tell where the ocean left off and the sky began. It was as though the elements had conspired to give Ricky and Vanessa perfection.

There was a path of small paper lanterns in a semicircle, and no sound could be heard save the crashing waves and the cries of gulls passing above. We followed them to the place where the boardwalk ended, all of us barefoot, to the place where the sand was just beginning to feel wet. We stood at the edge of the continent as small waves lapped at our feet, and gathered round Ricky and Vanessa.

Vanessa whispered something to Ricky, but I, standing closest, heard her ask him if he was ready. Her hand was shaking just enough for me to see that this was momentous for them. He just nodded and smiled at her. I don't think he could have spoken then. In his right hand, he held a silver weather balloon. He said, in a voice hoarse with emotion, "Goodbye, my beautiful Isabella," and released the balloon. Then he quoted something from Shakespeare, from "Hamlet", I think, "May flights of angels sing thee to thy rest." We all bowed our heads for a moment in silent prayer, then looked up as the balloon floated out over the Pacific, carrying the last remnants of Isabella's ashes.

There are few nights that are so indelibly etched in my memory. It was magical. The whole night seemed enchanted. Everything and everyone, all the love and friendships, the heartache and the joy seemed bathed in beauty… Evanescent beauty… That you couldn't hold in your hand, but you could feel in your soul.

I remember that night so perfectly because it was the night I was certain, beyond a shadow of a doubt, that Ricky was going to be fine. It was also the night my ragged heart began to heal.

THE END

T HANK YOU VERY much for picking up a copy of the novel Lost Pigeons! The reason my wishes are centered on writing this book is that I have been in silence for so many years about losing my brother.

I never thought that I could, or would want to, write a book capturing a terrible event interrupting my life. But, I did feel so obligated to break my silence and place my truth into such words, because I believe that maybe someone, some-where, is wondering why this is all happening to him or her; perhaps someone is in need of a brother or sister, and I hope that person will find solace!

I miss his presence so much since he left so tragically. That's when I started to express myself in small memos, doc-umenting what we did and didn't do together, as well as wish-es of what we could've done. I hoped to somehow heal the deep wounds of my soul and possibly help others in similar situations. It occurred to me that perhaps, my grief can trans-form another's into something of light and positive outcome.

This book is dedicated to all victims and survivors, but especially to those who have lost a loved one to suicide, ad-diction, an accident, or domestic violence. Needless to say, one shouldn't, and truly could never, forget the parents who read them bedtime stories and tucked them in, the childhood memories of brothers and sisters, or their own children that continue to suffer and endure oceans of pain and sorrow due to this magnitude of loss.

In my heart, I know that we can all find hope by stepping out of our comfort zones and lending a helping hand to our brothers and sisters out there who are struggling with demons that are greater than we'll ever know. This, to me, is one out of many roads toward peace and healing.

In loving memory of my brother Constantin Arau,
gone to soon but not forgotten!